For

Christmas 2002

with love,
Auntie Lori
+ (Jessica & Rachelle)

SUSAN SHREVE

▲ ▲ ▲

LUCY FOREVER, MISS ROSETREE,

——— *AND THE* ———

STOLEN BABY

▼ ▼ ▼

PICTURES BY ERIC JON NONES

TAMBOURINE BOOKS   NEW YORK

Library of Congress Cataloging in Publication Data
Shreve, Susan Richards. Lucy Forever, Miss Rosetree, and the stolen baby/by Susan
Shreve; illustrated by Eric Jon Nones. —1st ed. p. cm. Summary: Sixth-grader Lucy
Childs and her friend Rosie Treeman do not have much time for their pretend psy-
chiatric practice when Lucy's family decides to adopt a baby, who is kidnapped the
day after she arrives at their house. [1. Babies—Fiction. 2. Kidnapping—Fiction.] I.
Nones, Eric Jon, ill. PZ7.S55915Lu 1994 [Fic]—dc20 93-37187 CIP AC
ISBN 0-688-12479-8 (RTE)
1 3 5 7 9 10 8 6 4 2
First edition

To Molly Graham

chapter one

It was a gloomy Saturday afternoon in April and Lucy Childs, dressed as usual as Dr. Forever in her grandmother's old gray suit, high-heeled black suede shoes, and a strapless bra stuffed with pink toilet paper, was in a terrible mood. She sat at her desk in the offices of Shrinks, Incorporated—located in the basement of her house on Rugby Road in Charlottesville, Virginia—with a plate of Oreo cookies, licking the icing in the middle and waiting for something to happen.

No one was at home but Bolivar, the brain damaged cat, who lay beside Lucy on the desk and licked his yellow striped belly. Dr. and Mrs. Childs were on a drive in the country, which they usually did on Sundays, but this Sunday it was supposed to rain. They sat close to each other in the front seat, sometimes holding hands. Lucy imagined them whispering secrets back and forth which their first daughter, and only child for that matter, Lucy Darling Childs, known most afternoons as Dr. Forever of Shrinks, Incorporated, was not allowed to hear.

"You could come with us, darling," Mrs. Childs had said that morning before they left for the Blue Ridge Mountains. "We would love your company."

Lucy was always invited. But that meant riding in the backseat while her father, Dr. Childs—a well-known psychiatrist for children with serious problems—talked about wildflowers, and her mother—who painted landscapes in the third-floor studio of the Childs's house—talked about light and shadow, and Lucy Childs got sick swirling around the hairpin turns of the mountain roads.

"No, thank you," Lucy had said, when they asked her to go. "I have a lot of homework to finish in language arts and maybe Rosie is coming over."

Neither of which was exactly true. She did have homework in language arts, but she had no plans to do any homework at all until Monday morning. And Rosie Treeman, otherwise known as Miss Rosetree of Shrinks, Incorporated, was always busy on Saturdays and could not come over.

Rosie was the fifth child, second daughter, in a family of ten children who lived in a small house next door to the Church of the Immaculate Conception with her parents, her grandmother, her aunt, an old dachshund without any teeth, and ten goldfish, one for each child. Weekends, Rosie had chores and

6

church and family dinners and catechism, and Lucy Childs had absolutely nothing at all to do except her homework.

Lucy put Bolivar on the chair beside her and opened the manila folder on her desk.

Barnstone, Michael T., age 47, married. PROBLEM: Serious Agrophobia. (The definition of Agrophobia is fear of the outdoors.)

▲   ▲   ▲

Mr. Barnstone had lived in a closet in his bedroom for twelve years. The closet was empty except for a few old clothes and a telephone on which he spoke to Dr. Forever once or twice a day. Mrs. Barnstone brought his food on a tray and once a month or so she cleaned the closet, but she had to clean around Mr. Barnstone because he was even afraid to go into his own bedroom.

Lucy dialed the Barnstones' number on her telephone, which was a real telephone but not hooked up.

"Mrs. Barnstone," she said. "This is Dr. Forever of Shrinks, Incorporated." She lifted Bolivar onto her lap and let him lick the icing off her Oreo cookie. "I see. Well, tell him I hope he feels better." She hung up the telephone and put the Barnstone folder back in the file cabinet. Without Rosie Treeman,

7

she did not have the heart for Shrinks, Incorporated, today. In fact, she was so lonely, she wanted to crawl into her bed with Bolivar until Monday morning.

She wrote out DR. FOREVER, TEMPORARILY RETIRED and taped it to the front door of Shrinks, Incorporated.

Lucy had been known as Lucy Forever since the first day of nursery school at First Baptist, Main Street. When the teacher had asked a frightened and homesick Lucy what her last name was, she had said, "Lucy."

"I mean your last name," the teacher said.

"I'm Lucy Forever," Lucy had replied.

"Forever?" The teacher laughed.

"There's no such name," a little boy cried out.

"What is your real last name?" the teacher asked. "I know it can't be Forever."

And Lucy was too stricken to remember.

So Rosie, in a tiger-sized voice, said, "Her name is so Lucy Forever. I met her mother and she told me her name was Mrs. Forever."

And that was that.

Lucy did not like school, especially homework, and she always had detention in math for bad behavior, but at least there were other children at Haddenfield Elementary. And at home on Rugby Road, especially today, there was no one at all except Bolivar. Not even a dog, since Dr. Childs was allergic. Cinder, the child who Lucy and Rosie had rescued from the Albemarle County Home for Children, had been adopted by a family in Pittsburgh.

"I thought we were going to adopt Cinder," Lucy had said to her father, who had grown up in a very formal family in England and did not care for personal conversations about anything, including adoption.

Cinder had been a patient of Dr. Childs's who was brought to him when she suddenly refused to talk. Dr. Forever and Miss Rosetree had befriended her and discovered through their own detective work the reason why she refused to speak, and Shrinks, Incorporated, was in part responsible for saving her life.

"You promised we could adopt her," Lucy said.

"I did not promise, Lucy. You know very well I do not make promises I cannot keep," her father had said. "I told you we would try to keep Cinder if no one else could take her. And then the McGees wanted her very much."

But that night, when Mrs. Childs came in her bedroom—still painted cornflower blue for the baby boy the Childs's had expected when Lucy was born—Lucy could tell she was upset.

"I bet you miss Cinder too," Lucy had said.

"I do," her dreamy mother had said quietly. "I would love another child."

"Then you should be able to have one," Lucy had said, putting her head on her mother's lap.

"I can't, darling," Mrs. Childs said.

"We could adopt a baby."

"I wish we could, darling, but you know, your father and I are quite old to adopt a baby. I will be forty-two on my next birthday and your father is forty-six."

"So?" Lucy said.

"There are rules with agencies about older parents adopting—unless, of course, a baby just fell in our laps."

"Well, babies don't exactly fall in your lap," Lucy said crossly.

"Anything can happen," Mrs. Childs said, running her fingers through Lucy's hair.

But that was months ago and so far, nothing, not even a goldfish, had fallen in the Childs's laps.

Dr. Forever turned off the light on her desk, flung Bolivar over her shoulders, and walked up the basement steps to the kitchen. In the refrigerator was a bottle of Evian water, a loaf of eight-grain bread, old trout-and-broccoli from Friday's dinner, and a jar of natural peanut butter. She closed the refrigerator and called Miss Rosetree.

Mrs. Treeman answered the phone in her breathless voice, with the baby crying in the background and Ian, just two years old, saying, "No—no—no."

"Oh hello, Lucy," Mrs. Treeman said. "I'm sorry, but Rosie is helping at the church supper this afternoon."

"I thought she was probably busy," Lucy said sadly.

"But she may be able to come over tomorrow afternoon."

"Okay," Lucy said. "Thank you." And she hung up the telephone, went into the living room, and flopped face down on the couch, kicking off her mother's high heels.

Shrinks, Incorporated, wasn't exactly a game. It was actually a made-up business, but already by fall of last year, Dr. Forever and Miss Rosetree had had their first real patient when Cinder wandered into their offices. She'd been on her way to see Lucy's father, who worked in the old garage that he had converted into a doctor's office in the back garden on Rugby Road. Cinder was a real live patient, unlike Barnstone, Michael, age 47, who was one of the 468 imagined patients whose files were kept in the cabinet of the basement of the Childs's home on Rugby Road.

Every afternoon after sixth-grade classes at Haddenfield Elementary, Rosie Treeman packed her book bag and ran down University Avenue along the front of the University of Virginia where her father worked construction turning right at Rugby Road. She ran up the driveway marked by a wooden sign that read A.T. CHILDS, M.D. Just before she came to the small building where Dr. Anthony Childs had his office, she turned right and went through the door marked *Shrinks, Incorporated: Dr. Forever & Miss Rosetree*, into the basement now painted pale yellow and transformed into the offices of Shrinks, Incorporated. In the bathroom, where her clothes for Miss Rosetree were left hanging, she changed into one of Mrs. Childs's long wool dresses with a mandarin collar and a leather belt, put on panty hose which were quite large and brown leather high-heeled shoes, and got her eyeglasses and lipstick from the makeup box. Then she sat down at the desk next to the desk for Dr. Forever.

"Hello," she said, picking up the telephone. "This is Miss Rosetree of Shrinks, Incorporated." She listened. "No, I'm very sorry to say Dr. Forever is detained this afternoon at the hospital. I will have her call you as soon as she returns."

Which was usually at three-thirty after Lucy returned from detention.

Lucy Childs and Rosie Treeman had been best friends and business partners since nursery school at First Baptist. They had had a grocery store in Mrs. Childs's studio until Mrs. Childs discovered that they were selling real food and a large family of mice was happily reproducing baby mice on the shelves. Then they were veterinarians taking care of sick stuffed animals, until Lucy ate all the baby aspirin intended for the koala bear and had to have her stomach pumped. In the fourth grade, they started "Singers of the Dark of Night," playing rock music in the living room while Mrs. Childs worked in her studio and Dr. Childs saw children in his office. They spent hours choreographing dance routines, leaping from the French chairs to the living room couch to the coffee table until Dr. Childs said enough was enough. And then at the beginning of sixth grade, walking home from school one day, Lucy brought up the possibility of psychiatry.

"How would you like to be a shrink?" she asked Rosie Treeman.

"A shrink?" Rosie asked.

"Like my father," Lucy said. "We would take only serious cases. Like maybe a woman who has fallen in love with her German shepherd or a boy who thinks he's a bear."

Rosie was pensive. She had been very happy playing "Singers of the Dark of Night," especially since her mother did not permit anything but quiet games at her house and work, work, work. Besides, her father did not believe in psychiatrists.

"Either you go to church or to a psychiatrist," Mr. Treeman had said. "And church is cheaper."

"We could use the basement of my house and fix it up for offices," Lucy said. "My father says we can have his old desk, and I know we can borrow another one from my mother."

"What happens to the woman with her German shepherd?" Rosie had asked.

Lucy had rolled her eyes. "Well," she began. "She first tells her husband to move out and then she and her German shepherd move to an apartment, where she is very happy but the German shepherd is depressed."

"So he comes to our office?" Rosie asked.

"Right," Lucy said. "He comes to our office and you are his doctor."

Rosie began to smile.

"You tell him that in your opinion he would be happier with another German shepherd."

"So we'll both be doctors," Rosie said running her fingers through her short wavy hair.

"Of course," Lucy said.

"I was afraid I'd have to be a nurse."

"Not at all. I'll be Dr. Forever."

"And I'll call myself Miss Rosetree."

Soon the basement of the Childs house on Rugby Road was painted pale yellow. Mrs. Childs had given Lucy and Rosie her out-of-fashion dresses and skirts, her unused makeup and high heels, and Shrinks, Incorporated, opened its doors to patients not long after school started.

It was beginning to get dark. Lucy Childs was not exactly afraid to stay alone in the dark, but she didn't like it either. She particularly didn't like it on lonely afternoons when her mother and father were happily off on a drive in the country and Cinder had moved to Pittsburgh, Pennsylvania.

When it had turned completely dark and her parents were still not back, Lucy wandered through the house turning on the lights, with Bolivar draped over her shoulder. She was in the basement putting away the files for Shrinks, Incorporated, when the telephone rang in the kitchen. It rang several times before she got from the basement, up the steep steps, down the corridor next to the dining room, and into the kitchen. She was out of breath when she said, "Hello."

"Lucy," a very small voice whispered on the other end.

"Rosie? Is that you, Rosie?" Lucy asked.

"Guess what?" Rosie asked.

"I can't guess," Lucy said.

"I was at catechism and there was a church supper where I had to work, and Mrs. O'Brien who is a very nice nurse at the hospital was at the church supper with guess what?"

"I can't."

"Guess."

"I can't, Rosie," Lucy said. "A gorilla? A giraffe? A German shepherd?"

"Wrong, wrong, wrong. Guess again."

"I can't."

"A baby," Rosie said. "A six-day-old baby girl who was abandoned near the hospital. Mr. O'Brien heard her crying when he drove into the parking lot to pick up Mrs. O'Brien last night after work."

"Oh, brother," Lucy said.

"I told Mrs. O'Brien that your mother was waiting for a baby to fall in her lap and now there she is."

"Can I see her?" Lucy asked, her heart thumping.

But Rosie had to hang up because her mother was calling "Set the table," from the kitchen, and her father was calling "Dinner is ready."

So Lucy put the receiver back, took a handful of graham crackers out of the box, picked up Bolivar, and sat on the top step of the porch, waiting for her parents to return from the country to hear the news that something had finally happened.

chapter two

"No," DR. CHILDS SAID, HANGING HIS COAT UP IN the hall closet and taking off his boots, thick with red Virginia clay from a hike in the Blue Ridge Mountains. "Absolutely no." He turned on a reading light in the living room and sat down with one of his thick medical books about the problems of children.

Lucy leaned in the doorway with Bolivar draped across her neck.

"I'm sure you understand, Lucy," her father said.

Lucy nodded. "I didn't really think you'd agree."

Dr. Childs put on his glasses and settled into a chair. "But it was sweet of Rosie to think of us," he said.

"Rosie sometimes feels very sorry for me because I'm an only child," Lucy said.

"Everyone has one problem or another," Dr. Childs said. "Rosie Treeman, for example, might be very fond of the chance to be an only child."

"Well I'm not fond of it," Lucy said, and went into the kitchen where her mother had gone to cook dinner.

"There's nothing for dinner," Lucy said sadly, slipping into a kitchen chair to watch her mother examine the contents of a cupboard. "I checked."

"There's pasta," Mrs. Childs said.

"We always have pasta," Lucy said, but Mrs. Childs, too distracted with other thoughts to respond to the argumentative tone of Lucy's voice, turned on the gas burner under a pot of water and opened a box of spaghetti.

"Lucy." She slid into a chair across from her daughter and leaned over, speaking quietly. "Tell me exactly what Rosie said."

Lucy's heart leapt.

"Well," Lucy began. "Mrs. O'Brien's husband, who works with Rosie's father, found an abandoned newborn baby last night."

Mrs. Childs rested her chin in her hands.

"And did Rosie see the baby?"

"She did," Lucy said, trying to contain her excitement at her mother's interest. "She did. Mrs. O'Brien brought the baby to the church supper."

"And that's all you know?"

"I know it's a girl with peach-fuzz hair and a dimple on her chin. Rosie looked carefully at the baby. She didn't want to call us about any old baby, of course."

The water had begun to boil and Mrs. Childs dumped the spaghetti into the pot.

18

"I suppose that the mother couldn't cope, so she left the baby hoping someone would find it," Mrs. Childs said in her soft voice. "She's probably someone young, wouldn't you think, Lucy? Someone very young who doesn't know what to do with a baby." She took lettuce out of the bottom of the fridge.

"I didn't think about the mother," Lucy said truthfully. "I just thought about the baby."

"Maybe you could set the table," Mrs. Childs said. "The green mats and napkins. Ask your father if he'd like a beer with dinner."

"What I really thought about was how sweet she must be with a dimple," Lucy said, not wanting her mother to forget her sudden interest in this surprise baby.

Mrs. Childs smiled. "We had wanted another baby after you, but it never happened."

"What about Daddy?"

"Daddy too. Daddy especially wanted another baby."

"Well, he seems to have changed his mind now."

Mrs. Childs shrugged. "Maybe," she said. "But that was a long time ago. And we're both older than we were."

At dinner, Dr. Childs talked about the wildflowers he hoped to plant in the long expanse of land behind his office, and a new medicine which had proven quite successful in the treatment of childhood leukemia, and whether Mrs. Childs and Lucy would like to go to a film after supper.

"I can't," Lucy said, picking at her dinner. "I have homework."

"Homework?" Dr. Childs asked. "I thought you stayed home today because of homework."

"I have a lot of homework," Lucy said.

Perhaps she should mention the baby again. Perhaps she should tell her father about the dimple.

"I was actually thinking of working tonight," Mrs. Childs said. "I want to try to paint something I saw when we were walking today, darling. A strange old tree with exposed roots, the one I sketched."

"I particularly want to see this film," Dr. Childs said. "It's about the war, an educational film that Lucy would enjoy."

Oh, brother, Lucy thought, pouring more sauce on her noodles.

"It's a story of a Jewish man who pretended to be a German Protestant during the Second World War."

"Oh yes," Mrs. Childs said. "I read about that film." She served Dr. Childs more pasta. "You would like it, Lucy."

"What I would like to see is the baby with dimples and peach-fuzz hair," Lucy said.

There was a small silence, and then Dr. Childs swallowed his beer with a loud gulp.

"That would be an extremely bad idea," Dr. Childs said.

"Just to see her," Lucy said quietly. "Not to keep her."

"There's fruit," Mrs. Childs said brightly. "Bananas and apples and grapes. I could cut them up with some vanilla ice cream."

"Everyone in this family changes the subject," Lucy said.

"I'd love some fruit," Dr. Childs said. "No ice cream. What about you, Lucy?"

"Nothing," Lucy said glumly, and was just thinking of making a scene, of crying or storming off to her room or out the front door, when the telephone rang, and it was Mrs. Treeman.

"Hello, Mrs. Treeman," Mrs. Childs said brightly. "How are you and your family?"

"Good," Mrs. Childs said. "No spring flu this season?"

"Yes," she said.

"So I understand. Lucy mentioned it to us tonight."

"That's very thoughtful, of course," she said. "Certainly."

"Of course. Certainly." Dr. Childs got up clearing the dining room table.

"Let me talk to Dr. Childs and I'll call you back shortly, Mrs. Treeman," Mrs. Childs said.

Lucy sat in the chair in front of her half-empty plate of pasta and tried to disappear from view.

"There is no need to speak to Dr. Childs," Dr. Childs said, even before Mrs. Childs had hung up the telephone. "Dr. Childs says no."

"Darling," Mrs. Childs said, when she came back in the dining room.

"Absolutely no," Dr. Childs said.

"They have found the mother of this abandoned baby," Mrs. Childs said, sitting back down at the table next to Lucy. "That is what Mrs. Treeman was calling to say."

"Well, that's very good news," Dr. Childs said.

"Anthony," Mrs. Childs said, in the soft young voice she occasionally used with Dr. Childs to get her own way. "It's not necessarily good news. The mother is only fifteen years old, I believe—hardly even old enough to be called a mother—but the fact is, Mrs. Treeman called to let us know that the mother does not want the child."

"Evidently," Dr. Childs said. "Otherwise she wouldn't have left her."

"Anthony," Mrs. Childs began again, and Lucy slipped away from the table with her plate of pasta, went into the kitchen, and stood very quietly next to the stove, so she could overhear what her parents were saying and not be in the way.

chapter three

THE BABY WAS THE SIZE OF A LARGE DOLL LUCY TOLD Rosie later that night, after her parents had gone into their room, when she simply had to talk to Rosie Treeman in spite of the Treemans' rule about calls after 8:00 P.M.

She had soft yellow hair like the fuzz on the outside of peaches but longer, and dark blue eyes which she kept closed most of the time she lay wrapped in a pink hospital blanket on the Childs's white couch. She did not cry at all, as if she knew it was important, particularly for Dr. Childs, for her to be on her best behavior. Bolivar sat on the arm of the sofa biting the toenails on his paw, watching the baby girl.

Mrs. Belgrade, who was a social worker in private practice for Albemarle County, sat in the straight-back needlepoint chair beside the couch with her hands folded in her lap.

"So," she said to Lucy's father. "What do you think, Dr. Childs? She's quite beautiful, isn't she? That dimple! I love that dimple on her chin."

"She looks very much like a baby to me," Dr. Childs said. He was seated across from Mrs. Belgrade with *The New York Times* opened to the editorials. Lucy stood in the doorway, her arms folded across her chest, her heart beating in her mouth.

She did not know what her father was thinking, but she could tell that her mother had fallen in love with the new baby. Mrs. Childs sat on the floor next to the couch and played with the baby's fingers which were drawn into a tight tiny fist.

"She is lovely," she said to Mrs. Belgrade. "I suppose her hair will be blond," she said. "Anthony had blond hair, you know. For how long, Anthony? Until you were grown up?"

"Until I was five."

"And blue eyes," Mrs. Childs said. "May I pick her up?" she asked the social worker.

"Of course," Mrs. Belgrade said.

"She's a feather," Mrs. Childs said, as she picked the baby up. "So tiny. Lucy, have you ever seen anyone so tiny?" She held the baby against her chest.

"I spoke to the mother just this afternoon," Mrs. Belgrade began. "The story is this."

Lucy noticed that her father had lifted his head from *The New York Times* and was listening.

"Regina Blake. That's the name of the mother and she comes from Nelson County."

"How old is she?" Lucy asked.

"Fifteen—or fourteen, perhaps," Mrs. Belgrade said. "Dr. Caskie thought she was fourteen."

"I'm sure she wants money," Dr. Childs said. "She's probably got none at all."

Mrs. Belgrade nodded. "She wants some money, Dr. Childs. Not a great deal."

"I would have guessed," Dr. Childs said.

"Three thousand dollars is what she asked me for. Three thousand dollars and the amount of her hospital bill, because she is uninsured." Mrs. Belgrade went on.

"Buy a baby?" Lucy's mother said. "We would have to pay her for a baby."

"Exactly," Dr. Childs said. "It's an awful idea. I can't imagine purchasing a baby."

"She would of course like something to get on with her education," Mrs. Belgrade said. "This would be a private adoption."

"Explain a private adoption to me," said Mrs. Childs, sitting down on the couch with the baby resting in her lap.

Which Mrs. Belgrade did. If the Childses decided to adopt the baby girl and were willing to make an arrangement with Regina Blake through a written agreement with a lawyer, then in all likelihood the courts would allow them to adopt her legally. Otherwise, the baby would be placed through an adoption agency with parents who did not know the identity of her mother.

It was at that point that Dr. Childs asked Lucy to leave.

"Can't I just hold her once?" Lucy asked.

"No," Dr. Childs said. "You have homework."

"Just for a second, Anthony," Mrs. Childs said, handing Lucy the tiny bundle. "A feather, isn't she?" she said brightly.

"It was almost as if the blanket were empty," Lucy said to Rosie on the telephone. "And when I looked at her, she opened her eyes completely."

"So what do you think will happen?" Rosie asked.

"I don't know," Lucy said. "My father made me come upstairs so I couldn't hear them. I lay on my stomach at the top of the stairs trying to listen, but they had moved to the kitchen and all I could hear was my father saying in his fierce voice, 'I don't believe so.' "

Lucy was just telling Rosie Treeman about a private adoption when another receiver picked up and Dr. Childs said, "Lucy?"

"Yes, Daddy," she said.

"Please hang up the telephone and do your homework," Dr. Childs said. "Good evening, Rosie. Please give our best to your family."

"Good evening, Dr. Childs," Rosie said quietly.

Lucy climbed into bed still in her clothes and looked at her language arts assignment: "Read 'The Pasture' by Robert Frost and write a description of your own landscape." She tried to read again and again but she couldn't concentrate. She took out her notebook and wrote, " 'My Pasture' by Lucy Childs. My pasture is extremely small." She wrote, "The size of a baby." This she crossed out. "My sister Emily is extremely small." She crossed out Emily and wrote Sara, and then Elena and Jill and Kim. She started again. "My sister Pamela is extremely small." She had written one page front and back of names when she heard the clump of her mother's hiking boots on the stairs. She ran to the window, but was too late to see whether Mrs. Belgrade put the baby in her car before she got in and drove away.

"I was just finishing my homework," Lucy said, turning the pages quickly so her mother wouldn't see the list of baby names.

"Good, darling. You don't want to get any more detentions." Mrs. Childs sat down on the end of the bed holding crazy Bolivar up against her shoulder. She had a funny smile on her face.

"Did Mrs. Belgrade take the baby back?" Lucy asked.

Mrs. Childs was staring out the window into the dusk of early evening, and did not seem to hear.

"Mommy?" Lucy asked.

"I was thinking of the name Nell," Mrs. Childs said.

"Nell?"

"Didn't that little peach-fuzz of a baby girl seem like a 'Nell' to you?"

"Nell Childs?" Lucy's heart leapt into her throat. "Is that what you were thinking?"

"Or Emma," Mrs. Childs said. "Your Grandmother Childs's name. Mary Emma Childs."

"I love Emma Childs," Lucy said, throwing her arms around her mother's neck. "That's a beautiful name."

But before Lucy even had a chance to ask her mother where the baby was and whether Mrs. Belgrade had taken her, she heard her father's springy footsteps, and there he was in her bedroom with a familiar stern expression on his face.

"I told Lucy," Mrs. Childs said sheepishly.

Dr. Childs folded his arms across his chest.

"I was afraid you might have," he said. "But never mind."

"What do you think of 'Emma' for a name, Daddy?" Lucy asked.

"Emma Childs," Mrs. Childs said.

"I really hadn't thought we were so far along in a decision to give names," Dr. Childs said, taking a seat in Lucy's desk chair. "There is a great deal of legal work to be done and it's quite a big risk. We won't know if the child is actually ours for several months."

"That long?" Mrs. Childs asked.

"Anything can happen. Regina might decide she wants the baby back, which is her right until she is legally ours. The welfare agency might find us unfit parents because of our age. Particularly mine. Anything could happen, of course. So we can't get our hopes up."

"But she is lovely, darling, isn't she? You have to admit," Mrs. Childs said.

"Of course. She's a baby and babies are lovely. But even so, we might not get her, so we have to think sensibly."

"But you do like the name Emma, don't you?" Lucy asked, leaning against her father's shoulder.

"Yes," Dr. Childs said. "I like the name Emma very much."

chapter four

On MONDAY, THE LAST MONDAY IN APRIL AND RAINING
in sheets, Lucy Childs arrived home late as usual
after detention in language arts, with a report card
that had three C's, one B, and a note from Miss
Grace about Lucy's inattention in class. Her mother,
who usually painted all afternoon in her studio in
the old attic, was not at home. Instead a note on the
hall table said, "Lucy, sweet. I have an appointment
and will be back by supper. There are grapes in the
fridge and Oreos for snacks and please remind Rosie
her mother called to say she has a dentist appointment at 4:30."

Lucy slid her report card at the bottom of the stack
of bills and raced upstairs to change as usual into
Dr. Forever. She tossed her books on her bed where
Bolivar was sleeping, put on her mother's beige linen
skirt, a bra which she stuffed with toilet paper, and
an old silk blouse that was missing some buttons.
She piled her long thin hair on top of her head in a
lopsided bun, put on panty hose, her mother's patent

leather three-inch heels, and her wire-rimmed glasses without the glass. Then she hobbled down the steps to the offices of Shrinks, Incorporated, where Miss Rosetree was already dressed for the occasion and seated at her desk, talking on the telephone. Miss Rosetree gave a little wave.

Lucy opened the file drawer by the desk and took out the folder for Miss Azalea Greenhouse, with whom she had an afternoon appointment.

Greenhouse, Azalea, age 37, unmarried. PROBLEM: Miss Greenhouse is obsessed with plants. She has hundreds of them in her small apartment on Aiden Street. They fill the living room and bedroom and closets and kitchen. Recently Miss Greenhouse had to move into the bathroom and sleep in the tub. But then unfortunately her mother gave her a ficus tree for her birthday, and the only place to keep it is the toilet bowl. Even her car is full of plants, so there is hardly room for Miss Greenhouse to drive.

"I have to do something about my beloved plants,"
Miss Greenhouse said the first time she came in to see Dr. Forever. "They are ruining my life."

▲　　▲　　▲

Miss Rosetree put down the phone.

"Tartuffe died last night," she said sadly.

"Tartuffe?" Dr. Forever asked.

"Tartuffe," Miss Rosetree said. "Mr. Barton's

31

spider. Mr. Barton has had to be hospitalized for depression."

"That's terrible news." Dr. Forever sat down at her desk with Azalea's folder opened in front of her.

"I am going to call the spider company to get poor Mr. Barton a new spider," Miss Rosetree said.

"Good idea," Dr. Forever said, but she could not concentrate on Shrinks, Incorporated, this afternoon. She was too distracted even to read about Azalea Greenhouse. All she could think about was the baby—Emma Childs—maybe Mary Emma Childs after her father's mother. Emma Childs—the tiny perfect sister who was on her way, maybe this very moment, into her arms. And she must have sat for a very long time while Miss Rosetree was on the telephone with the hospital for Mr. Barton's depression and the spider company for his new spider, because the next thing Lucy knew, Rosie was shouting at her.

"Dr. Forever," she was saying. "Dr. Forever! Lucy! What is the matter with you?"

Lucy shrugged. "I forget," she said.

"Well, Azalea Greenhouse is here for her appointment."

"I guess she must be standing right in front of me and I can't see her," Dr. Forever said.

In front of Lucy was a desk, an empty chair, a

cement post painted yellow with *Dr. Forever's Office* written in black, and the basement door which led to the driveway—turn right to the office of Dr. Anthony Childs—turn left and walk down the driveway to Rugby Road.

"Hello, Azalea," Dr. Forever said to the empty chair. "I'm very sorry, but I was thinking of an emergency in my own family and forgot about you. Now you must tell me, have you been able to get rid of the ficus tree?"

She picked up the telephone. "This is Dr. Forever. I'm sorry. I'm with a patient. Please call me back at four-thirty."

"You do not look at all well, Azalea," Dr. Forever continued. "In fact, it looks as if your hair is falling out and clover is growing out of your ears, so you are going to have to get rid of your plants. The air in your house is probably full of invisible seeds, and you're swallowing them and breathing them in all the time. It's clear you are turning into a plant."

"Dr. Forever?" Miss Rosetree asked.

"I assume you can see that I'm speaking with Azalea Greenhouse, Miss Rosetree?"

"Of course I see that. I was the one who told you Azalea was here in the first place," Miss Rosetree said. "But your mother is calling."

"My mother is here?" Lucy jumped out of her

chair, kicked off her shoes, and ran up to where her mother was standing with Mrs. Belgrade, holding a bundle of blankets in her arms.

"Is that her?" Lucy asked. "Is she here to stay?" Lucy called Rosie to come upstairs right away.

"We hope she is," Mrs. Childs said.

The baby was sleeping, her eyes tight closed, her tiny fists drawn up to her chin, a soft down across her cheeks.

"Isn't she amazing?" Lucy said to Rosie.

Rosie looked at the small bundle.

"She's very nice," Rosie said.

"I guess you've seen so many of these in your house that you hardly even notice," Mrs. Childs said.

"I've seen a lot," Rosie said sticking her finger into the tiny fist. "But it's very good for you, Luce, 'cause you've never even had a chance to know what it's like. Besides," Rosie shrugged, "maybe this baby will turn out to be perfect."

"I doubt it," Mrs. Childs said, laughing. "But I want you to thank your mother for us. We're very glad to have the chance to have a new baby."

"It's just a chance?" Rosie asked, taking an Oreo cookie from Lucy.

"We can't be sure until the adoption is final," Mrs. Childs said. "There is quite a good chance. At least I hope it's a good chance."

The grandfather clock in the downstairs hall struck, and Rosie jumped up.

"I almost forgot," she said, running down the steps to the basement. "I've got to go to a dentist appointment."

Lucy followed her mother and Mrs. Belgrade upstairs into the bedroom that Dr. and Mrs. Childs shared. It was a large white bedroom with a small study in an alcove—overlooking the back garden—which had, since Lucy left for school in the morning, been turned into a small room for a baby with a straw bassinet and a changing table and a mobile with stuffed teddy bears hanging from the ceiling.

"I've been shopping for Emma," Mrs. Childs said, smiling.

Lucy sat down on the end of her parents' bed and took Emma in her lap. The baby's eyes fluttered. She made a little frantic motion with her hands before she turned her head against Lucy's belly and went back to sleep.

Mrs. Childs sat down on the couch and patted the seat for Mrs. Belgrade to sit down.

"We need to talk about just what it means to have Emma, Lucy, and I wanted Mrs. Belgrade to tell you about it."

Mrs. Belgrade was a very thin woman, quite pretty, with black velvet eyes, dark curly hair, and a starched white blouse flat as a board across her

chest. And she was nervous. She twisted the button on her suit jacket and kept her eyes downcast. Lucy remembered that later and remarked to Rosie about the way she picked the lint off her navy blue skirt and could not look at Lucy or Mrs. Childs.

"I wonder if you'd explain to Lucy about private adoptions," Mrs. Childs said. "You can tell her exactly what you told Dr. Childs and me."

Which Mrs. Belgrade did, explaining that Regina Blake, who was the mother of the new baby, was from a very poor family and was herself very young to care for the baby properly.

"Your parents have agreed to pay a little extra money to help Regina pay her hospital bill," Mrs. Belgrade said.

"But it will take some time before she is our baby by law, and in that time, Regina may change her mind," Mrs. Childs said.

"And then do we pay her more?" Lucy asked.

"No, no," Mrs. Belgrade said. "She will not change her mind."

"We hope," Mrs. Childs said. "But it is important to know, Lucy, that we are giving Emma a very good home now but she is not ours for keeps yet."

"But you think she will be, don't you?" Lucy asked.

"Of course I think she will be," Mrs. Belgrade said. She pushed her dark hair behind her ears.

"I don't know about Mrs. Belgrade," Lucy told Rosie later. Rosie called after having supper, doing the dishes, helping her little brothers with their homework, and setting her sister Maud's hair for a dance recital. "She seems a little weird."

"I'll tell you what's a little weird," Rosie said. "Very, very weird."

And she told Lucy about leaving the offices of Shrinks, Incorporated, that afternoon to go to her dentist appointment, turning right toward Rugby Road. And there, at one of the large rhododendron bushes that lined the driveway, was a man in Levi's and a blue shirt with a short reddish beard. But what was odd about him, actually unpleasant—besides the fact that he seemed to be spying—were his eyes, which she could feel burning through her as she walked past the bush.

"I would have called right away, but ever since I got home my father has been on the telephone with my uncle, and I was afraid to tell my mother what I'd seen. She might never let me go to your house."

"What do you think?" Lucy asked.

"I think somebody is watching you and did not expect me to come out of the house."

"Oh, brother, that's very bad news," Lucy said. "Things are almost perfect in my life and I don't want any trouble to happen now."

chapter five

THAT NIGHT DR. CHILDS AND MRS. CHILDS HAD A
terrible fight.

Lucy was lying in her small bed under the window
that overlooked Rugby Road. From time to time,
she could hear Emma's small baby sounds coming
from her parents' bedroom in the back of the house.
And then she heard her parents' voices. Quiet at
first, with her father's low voice and her mother's
soft musical soprano, always a little sleepy. And then
her father said, quite crossly and very loud, "That
is absurd, Caroline."

Lucy thought of "absurd" as a British word, and
her father used it often. But he never raised his
voice, and in particular, he had never—as far as Lucy
could remember—spoken crossly to her mother.

It was after midnight by the small alarm clock,
and Lucy slid out of bed. Her bare feet hit the
hardwood floors as she listened to the argument between her parents go on and on, becoming a fight.

"I don't wish to pay for a baby, Caroline," Dr. Childs said.

Lucy, standing in the hallway, could hear him clearly.

"This is bound to end badly for us and the poor baby if we pay these scoundrels any more money," he said.

"They aren't scoundrels," Mrs. Childs said. "They are poor people and we can afford to help them. Besides, they have only asked for a little money."

"Never mind. It feels like bribery, Caroline."

"At least, I want you to think about it," Mrs. Childs said.

"I'll think about it," Dr. Childs agreed.

The light in the hall was out, but the moonlight showed Lucy standing in her nightgown just beyond her parents' bedroom. And her mother saw her.

"Lucy," she said. "It's after midnight."

"You woke me up," Lucy said, scurrying back to her room.

"I'm sorry, darling," Mrs. Childs replied, following Lucy to her room.

Lucy crawled back under the covers and sat against her headboard.

"I've never heard you fight with Daddy before,"

Lucy said, her breath trapped in her chest and her cheeks too hot.

"We very seldom fight, Lucy," Mrs. Childs said.

"Is it about bribery?"

"Bribery?"

"Daddy said something about bribery."

"Yes, you're right. He did mention bribery," Mrs. Childs said. "We are concerned about that."

"I don't know what 'bribery' means," Lucy said.

"Your father is concerned that Regina and her family will take advantage of the fact that we want Emma so much, we are willing to pay them and pay them until the adoption is final."

"And is he right?"

"I don't know, Lucy. I just don't know." She lay down on the bed next to Lucy with the baby between them. "That's the trouble with getting your hopes up for a baby that might end up not to be your baby."

After her mother left, Lucy could not sleep. It began to rain and she could hear the rustle of raindrops on the roof and in the trees. But the rain did not make her sleep as it usually did. Emma woke up once in the night and cried, but someone picked her up. Lucy heard the shuffle of feet in her parents' bedroom, the lullaby sounds of her mother, and finally her father in his low, clipped voice saying. "Please, Caroline, turn off the light."

Perhaps, Lucy thought, a baby was a bad idea.

She watched the minute hand crawl around the face of the alarm clock between one and two o'clock, then between two and three o'clock, and sometime after three o'clock in the morning she fell asleep, sitting straight up in her bed. When she awoke to the sound of her mother's voice calling, "Breakfast," her head had fallen against the bedside table where Bolivar was cleaning his yellow paws.

"You only have ten minutes, Lucy," her mother called.

Her father was reading *The New York Times*, which he read at breakfast, but this morning he had a baby in his arm and he looked completely unfamiliar. Just to see him there—her serious English father, in his perfectly pressed tweed suit and a new baby resting sweetly against his chest—filled Lucy's heart with joy.

She slid into her chair and poured raisin bran into her bowl.

"Good morning, Lucy," Dr. Childs said.

"'Morning, Daddy." She poured milk on her cereal and took a piece of toast from the plate in the middle of the kitchen table.

"You must be tired this morning," Dr. Childs said. "It was late when you went to bed."

"I'm a little tired," she said, eating quickly so that she could be out of the house by 8:05.

"Well, I'm sorry about last night," Dr. Childs said. "I understand I woke you up."

"It's okay," Lucy said. "It's really fine." And she kissed her father and mother good-bye, then leaned over the soft bundle of yellow blankets and kissed Emma.

"Is Rosie coming to play Shrinks today?" her mother asked, as she packed a tuna fish sandwich for Lucy's lunch.

"Probably," Lucy said. "I mean she's coming over, but maybe we'll play with Emma instead." She flung her book bag over her shoulder.

"Then I'd like for you to baby-sit for a couple of hours while your father and I have an appointment with the adoption lawyer." Mrs. Childs kissed the top of Lucy's head.

"It's not actually baby-sitting," Lucy said, opening the kitchen door for Bolivar, who darted out the door. "I'm practically old enough to be Emma's mother."

"Almost," Mrs. Childs said, laughing.

On her way down the driveway to school, Lucy watched Bolivar drag a red object from under the rhododendron bush, throw it in the air as if it were a dead mouse, and dash back across the lawn. She picked it up, realizing that she had almost forgotten Rosie's call the night before. It was a red beard and mustache with a rubber band, the kind found in five-and-ten-cent stores at Halloween. Lucy slipped it into her book bag to show Rosie.

chapter six

Lucy and Rosie were in different sixth grade classes. Lucy was in Class 6 with Ms. Brooks, and Rosie was in Class 6X with Mr. Sears. Most days they did not see each other until recess on the upper field. And today Ms. Brooks, not known for her patience with children, asked Lucy to stay in during recess to finish her social studies project on the Navajo, in spite of the fact that her mother and father had gotten Lucy a new baby sister the night before.

"That shouldn't affect your homework," Ms. Brooks said. "You have too long a list of excuses, Lucy."

"Well it did affect my homework," Lucy said crossly.

She couldn't concentrate on her Navajo project. Her mind was spinning with the new baby, soft with the pleasure of a baby sister to come home to day after day—to walk in the carriage down Rugby Road, to teach to ride a two-wheeler, to tell about Santa Claus and summer vacation, to read to and play with on Christmas and Thanksgiving and the Fourth of July—to have her very own sister, not one of Rosie's which the Treemans let Lucy borrow for events like the Fourth of July picnic on the lawn of the University of Virginia.

But when the bell at the end of recess rang, Lucy had stopped thinking about Emma and was thinking instead about the red beard that Bolivar had discovered that morning, and which was now in the middle pocket of her book bag in her locker.

"I'm not quite finished," she told Ms. Brooks, when the teacher asked to see her social studies project. "I'll finish tonight. I promise."

"I certainly hope so," Ms. Brooks said.

Lucy wanted to be a good student. She wanted to have her name on the honor roll like Rosie Treeman, but there were so many other things she wanted to do even without a new baby in the house. And now, with Emma, it was going to be difficult to do any homework at all.

All of Tuesday moved so slowly, Lucy could hardly stand to look at the clock. The minute hand seemed to be stuck. In math class, she fell asleep and was sent to the bathroom to wash her face awake. In French, she forgot to say, "*Bonjour*, Madame Pierrot. *Comment ça va? Je m'appelle Lucy.*" And in gym they had to do relay drills in the hot gymnasium with the boys, because it had started to rain.

In fact, Tuesday took so long to go by that she had almost forgotten the red beard in her book bag, when she saw Rosie Treeman walking just ahead of her on Primrose Street and ran to catch up with her.

"Today was awful," she said, flinging a long slender arm around Rosie's shoulder.

"I heard," Rosie said sympathetically. "Sari said you had to stay in for recess to finish your social studies project. Didn't you tell Ms. Brooks about Emma?"

"Of course," Lucy said. "I wish I had Mr. Sears."

"He can be mean too," Rosie said sadly. "But not that mean. I doubt that Ms. Brooks likes babies."

"Or children."

"Probably not," Rosie agreed.

Lucy told Rosie about the red beard at TCBY Yogurt, where they shared a large French vanilla cone with granola at a table by the window.

"Oh, brother," Rosie said, her face pale. "That's creepy. We should tell."

"Tell the police?" Lucy asked, eating the granola from the top of the yogurt with her fingers.

"At least we should tell your parents," Rosie said. "We should tell them the whole thing. That I saw a man with a red beard hiding in the rhododendron bushes last night. And that this morning Bolivar found the red beard."

Lucy was pensive.

Already she was worried that her parents, especially her father, would decide to give Emma back. That she was too expensive, or too much trouble, or that they simply didn't want a baby after all.

"I'm worried about telling my parents, Rosie," she said thoughtfully.

"Worried about what?" Rosie asked, licking the last of the yogurt off her spoon and throwing the cone in the trash.

"If they think a man in a fake red beard has been watching our house, then . . ."

". . . They'll think it's about Emma," Rosie said, understanding Lucy's plight.

"Right." Lucy could feel tears gathering behind her eyelids. "They might even think he's the baby's father." She hardly ever cried: in fact, she was known at Haddenfield Elementary for not crying when other girls might. But already, she told Rosie as they left the TCBY Yogurt—Rosie's arm around Lucy's waist—even after one night, Emma was her baby sister and no one was going to take her away.

The Childses were at home when Lucy and Rosie arrived. Dr. Childs had cancelled his afternoon appointments to go to the lawyer's office to arrange for the adoption of Mary Emma Childs. Even Dr. Childs, normally dignified and reserved, could not contain his excitement.

"Mary Emma," Dr. Childs said. "Mary Emma for my mother," he explained to Rosie, whose family had long ago after ten children run out of family names. For the last three Treeman babies, they had chosen names from the pages of the *Charlottesville Daily Progress*. "She'll be very pleased." He lifted the baby from her new carriage to show her to Rosie.

"Now Luce," Mrs. Childs was saying, lining up the small bottles of Similac formula and the container of sterilized nipples. "You and Rosie will have to give up Shrinks, Incorporated, for today, if you don't mind, because we need you to take care of Emma."

"So we are going to keep her forever," Lucy said.

"Barring mitigating circumstances," Dr. Childs said, with his usual formality. And for once Lucy didn't even bother to ask what "mitigating circumstances" meant.

"We'll be fine," Lucy said. "Rosie knows all about babies."

"You do, don't you, Rosie?" Mrs. Childs asked, picking up her shoulder bag and putting on lipstick in the mirror over the hall table.

"Yes, I do," Rosie said tiredly, since, of course, she knew everything an eleven-year-old girl could possibly know about babies. More than she wished to know. "I know a lot," Rosie said.

"Well, good luck," Mrs. Childs said cheerfully.

And they were off.

Lucy stood with Rosie and watched her parents pull out of the driveway.

"It's a good thing we didn't tell them about the red beard," Lucy said. "They might have changed their minds about going to the lawyer's."

chapter seven

THE AFTERNOON WAS WARM FOR EARLY SPRING AND sunny, dappling the kitchen yellow. Lucy decided that she and Rosie should take Emma on a walk in her carriage down Rugby Road to Main Street, past the university, the candy shop, the bookstore, and the university students hanging around the street corners with their book bags and their cigarettes. But just before they got to the intersection of Main Street and Route 29, Emma began to cry in the high-pitched cry of a newborn baby, with tiny gasps and endless long periods of silence.

"Oh, brother," Lucy said.

"She's just hungry," Rosie said, not very much interested in an afternoon with a baby.

"Great," Lucy said. "I didn't bring any food."

"She'll be fine," Rosie said. "Let's just turn around and go home."

"Please," Lucy said. "She's going to stop breathing."

"Just jiggle the carriage a little," Rosie said. "I promise she'll be fine."

"Are you sure?" Lucy said. "It sounds like she's going to die."

"Positive," Rosie said. "Babies cry all the time and they almost never die of it."

Lucy flew up Rugby Road with the crying baby in the carriage and Rosie, not by nature much interested in hurrying, rushed along beside her.

"Now I don't know what to do," Lucy said, when they were back at the house and Emma was still making the most terrible sounds.

"Just this," Rosie said, opening the formula bottle and screwing on a sterilized nipple. She handed Lucy the bottle.

"No thanks," Lucy said. "You can do it."

So Rosie picked up the new baby, sat on the chair in the kitchen, and fed her a bottle. Emma drank happily until she fell asleep, while Lucy sat on the floor and watched.

"Babies are very easy," Rosie said, putting Emma back in her carriage. "They just eat and sleep, day and night, and nothing very interesting happens until they can walk."

Lucy poured cranberry juice into glasses and got out two chocolate chip cookies.

"So now what?" she asked licking the chocolate chips.

"Now she'll sleep for at least two hours," Rosie said. "So we can play Shrink."

"What about Emma?" Lucy asked.

"She'll be fine," Rosie said. "We'll be able to hear her if she cries."

So Lucy checked Emma sleeping on her stomach with her tiny fist in her mouth and ran upstairs, changing into her mother's old panty hose and patent leather high heels, her rose silk dress with a narrow belt, and her glassless eyeglasses. She tied her hair in a bun and put on wild cherry lipstick and blush.

"Miss Rosetree?" she called, coming down the steps.

Rosie was in the kitchen in a yellow linen suit tied around the waist to keep it up with one of Dr. Childs's old school ties. She wore pale pink lipstick, her curly mop tucked behind her ears.

"Oh, hello, Dr. Forever," she said.

"Hello, Miss Rosetree," Lucy said. "I see we're both a little late for work today. I have an appointment with Mr. Braintree. Remember? He's the man who refuses to leave the third grade, even though he was thirty-seven on January first."

"I have an appointment with the Major twins

today. They will wear only one dress, but unfortunately they both can't fit into it at the same time."

They walked down the basement steps to the Offices of Shrinks, Incorporated, leaving the baby sleeping in her carriage in the kitchen.

Dr. Forever picked up the telephone. "Hello, Mr. Rubin. This is Dr. Forever." She paused. "Why that is wonderful, absolutely wonderful. I'll bring over three hundred dollars right away." She sat down at her desk.

"Three hundred dollars for what?" Miss Rosetree asked.

Dr. Forever turned around. "I didn't tell you earlier because I was afraid things might not work out, but I have adopted a baby girl."

"A baby girl?" Miss Rosetree exclaimed. "That is wonderful for you, Dr. Forever."

"It's a special adoption," Dr. Forever said. "And it costs quite a bit of money."

"Three hundred dollars?"

"Exactly," Dr. Forever said.

"Well, I'm very glad for you Dr. Forever, but I'm sorry to say I doubt I will ever adopt a baby or have a baby myself or even get married." She picked up the telephone and dialed. "Hello, Mrs. Major. This is Miss Rosetree. I am too busy to see the twins today. But I suggest you tell them that you are going to cut the dress in half and that each one can wear half a dress to school. Thank you very much." She put down the telephone. "I love living in my very own apartment, without anybody messing up my room."

Lucy stood up. "Did you hear something, Rosie?" she asked, putting her finger to her lips for quiet.

"I don't think so," Rosie said. "But maybe you should check."

And Lucy ran up the stairs to check.

Emma was sleeping, making sweet cooing sounds in her throat, her eyelids quivering. Lucy leaned down and kissed her tiny fist.

"She's still sleeping," Lucy said, when she went back downstairs.

"They sleep for hours when they're newborn," Rosie said, dialing the telephone. "I need to put Mrs. Astor in the hospital to be fumigated," she said. "Poor Mrs. Astor is so convinced she's a Labrador retriever that she has developed fleas. Hello," she said. "This is Miss Rosetree of Shrinks, Incorporated, and I need a room for Mrs. Astor."

"Now I do hear something," Lucy said.

"It's the doorbell," Rosie said. "I hear it too."

"I'll get it," Lucy said.

"Could you bring some more chocolate chip cookies when you come down?" Rosie called, as Lucy dashed up the steps.

A young man in khaki pants, with a suit jacket and tie and long sandy hair cut in bangs across his forehead, stood at the door with a handful of pamphlets.

"Hi," Lucy said.

"Hello," the man said pleasantly. "I am Mr. Barnes, collecting for the Heart Fund. You must be Dr. Childs's daughter."

"I am. I'm Lucy, and they're out right now."

"Well, I spoke with your parents yesterday and they asked me to come back this afternoon to collect. Any amount will be greatly appreciated."

"Just a moment," Lucy said. "We have to be a little quiet because my baby sister is sleeping in the kitchen."

"Of course," Mr. Barnes said. "Your parents told me yesterday you have a new baby sister."

Lucy smiled. "Her name is Emma," she said. She started up the steps to her room. "I don't have much money," she said.

"What is important is that everyone gives something," Mr. Barnes said. "Not how much you give."

"I mean I have less than twenty dollars, I think," Lucy said.

"I'll be happy with that," Mr. Barnes said, smiling warmly.

"Okay," Lucy said. "Just a sec. I'll go get it." She ran up the front steps past Bolivar, who was slowly meandering down the steps. She kept her allowance in her top dresser drawer next to her jewelry box, in a box of treasures, along with shells from the beach, a sixpence from her English grandmother, her Great-aunt Lucy's locket, and a silver dollar. There were four one-dollar bills, a five, a ten, and eight cents in change. She took three single bills. Halfway across the room, she changed her mind and returned the three dollars, taking the five-dollar bill instead.

Bolivar was lying on the rug beside the front door, cleaning his paws, and the front door was closed, not completely, but ajar. Lucy opened the door and Mr. Barnes was no longer there. She stepped outside onto the front porch and did not see him. Then she walked down the front steps, clear down the driveway to Rugby Road, feeling strangely uneasy. He was nowhere to be seen.

Rosie was at the front door when Lucy came back up the driveway.

"What happened?" she asked.

"A man came collecting for the Heart Fund," Lucy said. "But when I came downstairs with the money, he was gone."

"Where did you put the baby?" Rosie asked.

"The baby?" Lucy said, her heart in her mouth. "The baby is in her carriage."

Rosie, white-faced, shook her head. "Not any longer," she said to Lucy. "The carriage is empty."

chapter eight

Mr. BARNES WAS GONE.

Mrs. Dryer, next door to the Childses, told Lucy she had seen an unfamiliar car parked in front of her house, a large robin's-egg blue car, very old, with a dent in the driver's side. The car had been there when she was bringing in the groceries but it was gone now. She had not seen a sandy-haired man in a khaki-colored suit, and no one had been to her house collecting for the Heart Fund. On second thought, Mrs. Dryer said, someone had been in the car. A woman was seated in the front seat, hiding her face in her hands as if she were weeping.

"Why do you want to know about this man, Lucy?" Mrs. Dryer was always too curious about the Childs's lives. "Did he do something he shouldn't have done?"

"He might have," Lucy said in a shaky voice,

unwilling to tell Mrs. Dryer what had really happened, too ashamed and frightened to even speak the words, "stolen baby."

But Rosie told the police the whole truth when they arrived with two cars, one unmarked with a plainclothes officer who got out of the car just as Lucy was coming up the driveway. In the police car were two officers, one of them a woman who, when she saw the stricken look on Lucy's face, put her arm around her shoulders.

"I'm very sorry," she said sympathetically.

"It's all my fault," Lucy was crying now. "I was so completely stupid."

"We'll take care of it," the officer said. "You can help us by giving us all the information you can possibly remember."

Rosie was the one who gave the information. Lucy couldn't talk. She sat on the couch next to Rosie, her hands folded in her lap, certain that she was going to be sick.

Rosie told the police the story from the start, about the baby and how the Childses were going to adopt her in a private adoption which was going to cost quite a lot of money, about the man in the red beard who had dropped his beard beneath the rhododendron bush, and about Mr. Barnes pretending to collect for the Heart Fund.

"Do your parents know about the man with the

red beard?" the policewoman asked.

Lucy shook her head.

"Why not?"

"I was afraid that if they knew someone was hiding in our bushes, they'd change their mind about keeping Emma," Lucy said quietly.

"You should have told them," the plainclothes detective said.

"I know," Lucy said. "Now I know."

"We sort of forgot," Rosie said. "Just after I saw him, I told Lucy. And then later, the next day, she found the beard. We talked about telling the Childses, and then today, I just forgot."

"Me too," Lucy said. "Or I would have been suspicious about Mr. Barnes."

"Did Mr. Barnes look at all like the man in the bushes?"

"I don't know. I didn't see Mr. Barnes, and Lucy didn't see the man in the bushes. All I know about the man is that his hair was red."

"Mr. Barnes had brownish hair, and he was tall and quite young," Lucy said.

The detective, who was taking down the information in his notebook, looked up.

"You said there was money involved in the adoption of this baby?"

"Three hundred dollars," Rosie said with confidence.

"No, not three hundred dollars," Lucy said quickly. "What I overheard my father say was in the thousands."

The detective gave the police officers a look.

"My guess is we will hear from Mr. Barnes again," he said.

"Hear what?" Rosie asked.

But the detective did not reply, because the Childs's car had pulled into the driveway.

"Lucy?" Mrs. Childs called out breathlessly. "Are you all right? What are the police doing here?"

But before Dr. and Mrs. Childs came into the living room, Lucy bolted. Out through the dining room, the back hall, the kitchen—tripping over Bolivar lying in the middle of the kitchen floor—and out the back door.

At the driveway, by the rhododendron bush, she stopped. She was still dressed as Dr. Forever and did not want to be seen walking down Rugby Road in high-heeled shoes and lipstick. She did not want to be seen by anyone and she didn't want to talk, so she climbed under the huge bush where Mr. Barnes—at least probably Mr. Barnes—had been seen by Rosie Treeman the night before. Her mind was spinning.

She imagined Emma in the back seat of the blue car, flying back and forth as Mr. Barnes drove too fast out of Charlottesville. The hungry baby was crying and crying, her small bottles of Similac still lined up on the kitchen counter.

Maybe they would harm her, Lucy thought. If she continued to cry like she had earlier, maybe Mr. Barnes would lose his temper and spank her. Maybe he'd bury her in the woods just outside Charlottesville and Lucy would never see her again. And then what? How would Lucy ever be able to face her mother and father or go to school or play in the offices of Shrinks, Incorporated? Or sleep again? Or eat, ever?

She could not bear the sadness.

For a long time, she sat under the bush in a thick web of rhododendron leaves. Twice her father came out and called to her. The police officers left, and after that her mother walked down the driveway calling, "Lucy, Lucy," in a weepy voice. Finally the detective left, walking toward Rugby Road with Dr. Childs. They were talking, but Lucy could not understand what they were saying.

The sky was beginning to darken when Rosie finally came out. Lucy lay next to the large trunk of the bush with her eyes closed, but she was not sleeping. Rosie walked down the driveway and stopped at the bush, her feet planted very close to Lucy's face.

"Luce?" she said softly.

Lucy didn't reply.

"Lucy, I know you're there." She leaned through the branches of the bush and touched Lucy on the head.

"Your parents aren't mad at you," Rosie said.

"I don't care," Lucy replied, without opening her eyes.

"The detective thinks we're going to find her," Rosie said.

"If we do," Lucy said, "she'll probably be dead."

"You can't think that way, Lucy," Rosie said. "You have to believe we'll find her."

"Well, I don't," Lucy said.

Rosie crawled into the bush and sat down next to Lucy under the tent of leaves. "I have to go home pronto, but call me tonight and I'll tell you my idea." She hugged Lucy's slender shoulders. "I promise we'll find her, Lucy."

Lucy lay on the ground and watched the day disappear. The sky grew black, the sun fell completely beyond the trees. Eventually she would go inside. After the lights were out downstairs and her parents had gone to their bedroom, then she would go in the back door, slip downstairs to the offices of Shrinks, Incorporated, and sleep—if she possibly could sleep—on the couch. From time to time, her father came out and called to her. But Lucy guessed rightly that Rosie had telephoned to tell them that she was safe in the rhododendron bush, and they had decided to let her stay there.

She must have fallen asleep with exhaustion because the first thing she heard was a car pull up on Rugby Road and stop at the end of the driveway. It was almost eleven. Someone in trousers, she could not tell if it was a man or woman because the streetlight lit only the trousers from the ground where she was lying. But someone was slipping something inside the Childs's mailbox, and before she had a chance to sit up, the person had jumped into the car and driven away.

chapter nine

Put $3,000 in cash in the mailbox marked Kroger on Route 29 just beyond Stamans' Drugs at 8 p.m. Saturday, or you'll never see the baby again.

The note from the mailbox sat in the middle of the dining room table, while Dr. and Mrs. Childs waited with Lucy for the police and the detective to arrive.

"Are you quite certain you can't identify the car?" Dr. Childs asked Lucy.

"Positive," Lucy replied in a thin, irritated voice. "It looked like every other car in the dark."

"Of course," Dr. Childs said absently. "Would you like some more tea, Caroline?" he asked his wife.

Mrs. Childs shook her head.

"I would recognize the man who called himself Mr. Barnes," Lucy said. "Even if he were wearing a wig. I would know his face."

"Well, that may be very important," Dr. Childs said, getting up to put on water for tea.

"Why didn't you mention the red beard to us?" Mrs. Childs asked.

"I told you," Lucy said crossly. "I've already told you twice. I thought you'd change your mind about the baby if I told you there was a man in the bushes in a fake red beard watching our house. I thought it was probably the father of the child checking us out."

"Let's drop that subject, Caroline," Dr. Childs said, coming in with a plate of cookies and tea.

"I certainly didn't think the man in the bushes was dangerous," Lucy said. "Or I wouldn't have waited to tell you."

Dr. Childs ruffled her hair. "Have some tea, darling, and you'll feel better."

"Right," Lucy said. "Just a cookie and a little tea and I'll be fine." She got up from the table and picked up Bolivar from the floor, where he was cleaning his face. "I just knew that at the first sign of trouble, like the news of a man hiding in our bushes, you guys would say okay, no baby. And I wanted a baby."

The detective was not surprised to read the note which had been left in the Childs's mailbox. "I was certain this would happen," he said. "He knows you have enough money to pay for this baby, so he steals her and tries to force you to pay him."

"So of course we do that," Mrs. Childs said. "That is what we'll do, isn't it, darling?"

"Of course," Dr. Childs said.

But the detective was pensive.

"We do have an officer posted on the road near the Blakes to watch for suspicious activity, and we're trying to locate the social worker Mrs. Belgrade," he said. "But this is tricky business. I've had only one other ransom for a kidnapping, and it didn't work."

"What happened?" Lucy asked.

"I always think the best thing is to put the money where you've been told to put it, and wait someplace nearby but concealed from the kidnapper," the detective said, ignoring Lucy's question.

"Did the child in the other case get killed?" Lucy asked.

"Lucy," Dr. Childs said.

"I want to know," Lucy told him.

"We never found her," the detective said.

"So you assume she was killed?" Lucy asked.

"The plan didn't work," was all the detective was willing to say.

Nevertheless, it was decided by the Childses and the police and the detective that Dr. Childs leave the house, drive out on Route 29 beyond Staman's Drugs, and place three thousand dollars in the mailbox marked "Kroger." He would then drive back home while the detective would park his unmarked car not far from the mailbox and wait for someone to come pick up the money.

"It will be almost dark and difficult to see," the detective said. "But it's worth a try."

"The point is," the policewoman said, "that if the plan works, the kidnapper will lead us to the child."

"What you worry about is frightening the kidnapper," the detective said. "And then he could do harm to the baby."

That night Lucy did not sleep at all. She saw the sun slide over the horizon like a pale yellow plate, casting a long slender line of light over her bed. And then, at seven o'clock the next morning by the alarm clock on her bedside table, just when she knew all of the Treemans were out of bed, she called Rosie.

"I need your help," she said.

"For what?" Rosie asked.

"The police need everything possible to help them find the baby."

"I'll call right back after breakfast." Rosie said.

"You have told them everything, haven't you, Lucy?" Mrs. Childs asked later when Lucy had come downstairs for breakfast.

"Everything," Lucy said. "I'm sorry we didn't tell you about the man in the bushes."

"Never mind, Lucy," her father said.

"And I'm not going to call any of my friends to play today. I'll just go back to bed with Bolivar until they find her."

Dr. Childs gave Mrs. Childs one of his looks of exasperation, but neither of them said anything.

"And if anyone calls, I'm not here," Lucy said, going upstairs. "Except Rosie." But she did not go to bed. Instead she went to her parents' bedroom, where the bassinet sat in the window. She carried it into her own bedroom, putting Bolivar on the new white and yellow quilt, and waited for Rosie to call.

chapter ten

EVERYONE CALLED ON SATURDAY MORNING BUT ROSIE.
Even Mrs. Treeman.

She called to say she had heard the terrible news
about Emma and had just gotten information from
the priest at her parish who knew Regina Blake. "I'll
be over right away," she said.

But she did not come over right away at all. By
lunchtime, when Mrs. Childs tried to make Lucy
eat a tuna fish sandwich, Mrs. Treeman still had not
appeared.

"I wish she hadn't promised to come," Dr. Childs
said crossly. "Then we would not have gotten our
hopes up."

"She'll come, darling," Mrs. Childs said. "Mrs.
Treeman is a very dependable woman, and I'm sure
if she has important news she'll let us know."

Other people came. Two men from the *Charlottes-*
ville Daily Progress arrived in the afternoon, hoping
to interview the Childses, who were in Dr. Childs's
office talking to the police. So Lucy answered the

door. She told the reporters everything, all about Mr. Barnes and how Rosie had seen a man with a red beard that turned out to be a fake. She was just beginning to tell the reporter how desperate she had been for a baby, when Dr. Childs walked up the path.

"We don't want any stories in the paper until we're clear about the fate of this child," he said to the reporter, in his familiar cool British accent.

"Of course, sir," the reporter said. "We understand."

"Did you answer any questions, Lucy?" he asked in a snappish voice.

Lucy was just about to confess that yes, she had answered quite a lot of them, when the reporter shook his head.

"I just arrived, Dr. Childs," he said. "I haven't had the opportunity to ask any questions."

"There will be no story in the newspaper at all," he said. "Not even a notice that the baby has been kidnapped."

"It could frighten Mr. Barnes," Dr. Childs said, checking the growth on his rosebushes as if this Saturday were a perfectly normal day. "And if he's frightened, he could harm Emma. So you were wise not to say anything to the reporter, Lucy."

Later, in the kitchen with her mother—after the Gradys from next door had brought over a casserole for dinner, and the McLeans from the house behind the Childses and Dr. Alistair from the University had come to call, as well as Monica and Sarabelle from Haddenfield Elementary—Lucy started to tell her mother about the reporter. But before she could finish the story, the telephone rang, and it was Rosie.

"Luce," Rosie said, in a stage whisper. "Something's happened. Meet me on your bike at the corner of Main and Route 29. Now. I've found out where Regina Blake lives. And hurry."

Lucy's blood was racing. She put down the phone.

"That was Rosie," she said.

"I know it was Rosie," her mother replied.

"She wants to meet downtown," Lucy said, hoping her voice did not betray her excitement.

"That's lovely for you, sweetheart," Mrs. Childs said. "The day will seem shorter with something to do."

The telephone rang and it was Rosie again.

"Luce," she whispered. "My mother is on her way over to your house to tell your parents what she found out from Father Matthew. So if you see her, don't tell her you're meeting me, because I told her I was taking cookies to the Retirement Home."

Usually Rosie Treeman was the less adventurous member of Shrinks, Incorporated: sweet, studious, dutiful, and loyal. Lucy was usually the one with great plans.

"That was Rosie again," Lucy said, running up the stairs to get her baseball cap, which she put on backward, and a rubber band for her long, thin, flyaway hair. "She is taking cookies to the Retirement Home and I'm meeting her there."

When she came down, Mrs. Childs kissed her forehead. "Be careful on your bike, Luce," she said as usual.

"I'll be fine," Lucy said, worried that her mother might change her mind and not allow Lucy to take her bike.

That morning, after the ten o'clock Mass, Father James had come over to the Treemans' house to talk to Mrs. Treeman about Regina Blake. At the time, Rosie was in the kitchen helping her mother make a macaroni salad for supper, so she stayed there, cutting up celery and onions, listening to Father James.

Father James was the kind of busy priest who made the personal lives of the less fortunate people in Charlottesville his business. Since the appearance of the abandoned infant, the baby and her mother had been Father James's first priority. In questioning people in his parish, he learned about Regina Blake and had gone to Baker's Hollow, where she lived, to explain what it would mean to give up her baby. Regina said that was all right with her, since she hadn't even planned to have a baby. She had three more years of high school left and didn't know how she could take care of a baby and go to high school, since her mother worked all day at K Mart and her sisters were in elementary school. When he asked her about the father of the baby, she said he was not a very good man and couldn't be expected to help out.

"What do you mean 'not a good man'?" Father James had asked.

"I mean bad," Regina had said.

"I suppose that that was the man who came to the Childs's house collecting for the Heart Fund," Mrs. Treeman had said, after Father James left.

"I'm sure it was," Rosie replied, dumping the chopped onions and celery in the bowl of macaroni.

"And he probably is the one who took the baby, because he knew there was money to be had from the Childses in getting the baby back, since they live in such a big house and would be willing to pay." Mrs. Treeman washed her hands, cleaned peanut butter off two-year-old Ian's face, and fed the baby applesauce. "I'm going to call Caroline Childs right away and go over to tell her about this," Mrs. Treeman said, dialing the Childs's number.

Rosie finished feeding the baby its applesauce, folded the morning papers that her father had left all over the floor, and checked the chicken in the oven, all the while listening to her mother's conversation.

"Where is Baker's Hollow?" she asked, when Mrs. Treeman got off the phone.

"You are not going to Baker's Hollow, Rosemary," her mother said. "You can put that out of your mind right now."

"Of course, I'm not going, Mama," Rosie said. "I just wondered where it was, since I never heard of it."

"You can wonder all you like, but you and Lucy Childs keep your investigating business in the Childs's basement and don't get yourself in trouble like you did with that poor child Cinder."

Rosie was making plans to call Lucy Childs, to arrange to ride their bikes to find Regina Blake.

"I'm going to take cookies to the Retirement Home after lunch," she said.

"That's a lovely idea," Mrs. Treeman said, taking the chicken out of the oven. "Maybe you could take Ian with you."

"I can't," Rosie said. "Maudie can take care of Ian for a change. I'm riding my bike."

After lunch, after Mrs. Treeman went with leftovers for her mother and auntie who lived around the corner, Rosie called the Charlottesville operator to ask how to find directions to a place outside Charlottesville called Baker's Hollow.

As it happened, the operator knew Baker's Hollow very well.

"Out Route 29," she said. "Past Barracks Road and the K Mart. Turn right on the second dirt road marked Route 833," the operator said. "It's not much of a place."

"That's okay," Rosie said, and she dialed the number for Dr. Forever.

chapter eleven

THE AFTERNOON WAS HOT FOR APRIL AND AIRLESS.
The uphill trip on bicycles was long—much longer
than Rosie, who was a little plump and not athletic,
had imagined. By the time they finally reached
Route 833, she was out of breath and had to sit down
on a rock for quite a long time before she was ready
to try the bumpy, narrow road back into the woods.
Small signs with names—*Marray, Shifflett, Morris*—
were marked along the road. A piece of painted
wood, with *Blake* in red magic marker, was nailed
to a tree.

"I'm sort of scared," Lucy said, getting off her bike.

"Me too," Rosie said.

They were in a thick grove of trees on a dirt path,
wide enough for a car. There were no houses but
there were abandoned cars, and pickup trucks on
blocks, and dirt paths branching off and marked by
the names of families. It was dark and still under
the trees, with a sense of foreboding in the quiet as
if a storm were gathering.

"It's creepier than I thought it would be," Lucy said.

"Let's go back," Rosie said quickly. "I think I'm going to be sick."

"You're not going to be sick, Rosie Treeman," Lucy said, feeling stronger. "We've already almost died of exhaustion getting out here," she said. "Nothing is going to happen now."

"Unless he's here," Rosie said, sliding her hand in Lucy's.

"Well, he's not," Lucy said. "I can't imagine that he's here. He's got to be in hiding."

"Do you think the baby is here?" Rosie asked.

"Maybe," Lucy said. "That's what I'm hoping."

Walking their bikes, they came to the path marked *Blake*.

The path was long and curved back into the woods, with large roots along the narrow ribbon of dirt and beer cans along the side of the road. From time to time, they stopped and listened.

"I can't believe we haven't come to anything yet," Rosie said.

"Shh," Lucy said, stopping, putting her hand over Rosie's mouth.

They listened.

"Do you hear?" Lucy whispered. Rosie nodded.

They heard voices—not just conversation. It

sounded more like singing. Then a man's voice, not harsh, but loud and rolling Southern, said, "Now what did you do that for, Constance?"

"I don't want to go if there's a man," Rosie said, ducking behind a tree. "I thought we'd only see Regina Blake," she said. "Otherwise I wouldn't have come."

"It was your idea to come," Lucy said, no longer so frightened, her heart pounding with excitement now. "And you said yourself, Regina is only fifteen years old—so it's not likely she lives out here by herself."

"Maybe she's fifteen," Rosie said. "Old enough to have a baby."

"Then that man is probably her father and Constance is maybe her mother," Lucy said, leaning against the tree.

"Maybe," Rosie said, sinking to the ground, crawling under a low broad-leaved bush. "Lucy?"

Lucy knelt down beside her.

"I'm just too scared," she said. "You go to the Blakes's and I'll stay here and warn you if someone comes."

Lucy considered. "Okay," she said, "I'll go a little way more." She gave a little laugh. "As long as I don't see him."

"Be careful," Rosie whispered, as Lucy started down the path toward the sounds of the voices.

Lucy could still hear them, particularly the man. And he did sound angry as she moved closer. There was a strong sweet smell coming from somewhere just beyond her and the smell of smoke.

The path was much longer than she had thought it would be, especially with the sounds of voices so close. And darker. From time to time she stopped to listen, but she was not aware of anyone else on the road until a voice behind her said, "What are you doing on my road, girl?"

The blood went out of Lucy's legs. Her mouth was dry and she closed her eyes, too frightened to turn around.

The voice belonged to a woman, maybe a girl. But when Lucy did look behind her, no one seemed to be on the path. Although certainly she could feel a presence somewhere, as if the voice came from the ghost of a girl and not a real girl at all.

"What did you say?" Lucy asked, turning to face where the sound had come from, her slender arms folded across her chest.

There was a long silence. And then a young woman, heavyset with a round, almost sweet, face and a tooth missing right in the front, her hair pulled back in a long braid, stepped out from behind a tree.

"I asked you what you were doing on my road," she said, holding her braid, slapping her cheeks with it nervously.

"I'm looking for a woman named Regina Blake," Lucy said, hoping her voice had a confidence she did not exactly feel.

"What for?" the young woman asked.

"I need to talk to her," Lucy said.

The woman shook her head. "What would a girl like you want with Regina Blake?" she asked, shifting her body so that one hip was up. "What you are really looking for is Regina's baby, isn't that right?"

She took a cigarette from the pocket of her blue jeans and lit it. "I suppose you don't want a cigarette," the woman said.

"No thank you," Lucy replied. "I don't smoke a lot."

"Well," the woman said, cocking her head with an odd expression on her face. "I got bad news for you." She took a long drag on her cigarette and blew the smoke into the leaves just over her head. "Regina Blake's baby is disappeared."

Lucy's heart stopped.

"She may be dead." She rubbed the lit end of the cigarette against the tree, dropped it on the ground, and headed beyond Lucy along the path.

"Did you hear that?" Lucy asked when she reached the place where Rosie was still hiding.

Rosie shook her head.

Lucy sank down on the ground next to her.

"I saw the girl pass by me when I was hiding under the bush," Rosie said. "Was that Regina Blake?"

"Maybe," Lucy said. "She didn't say."

She didn't tell Rosie what the woman had told her about Regina's baby. At the moment, she could not bear to say it.

"Let's get out of here," Lucy said.

They took their bikes and hurried down the path to the main dirt road and a clearing where the sun dappled the road with light.

"I can't ride back," Rosie said.

"Of course you can," Lucy said impatiently, her throat tight, her head spinning.

"I almost fainted, Lucy. I really can't," she said. "You go on. I'll walk."

Lucy climbed onto her bike.

"It'll take days to walk," she said to Rosie. "Stop being so scared."

"I'm not scared," Rosie said, her eyes filling with tears. "I'm just too tired. Anyway," she said, "I hate Shrinks, Incorporated. I'm never going to play again."

On Route 29, she climbed onto her bike. "We always have these terrible things happen," she said.

"What happened this time has nothing to do with Shrinks, Incorporated," Lucy said crossly. "As you very well know, you called me to say that a baby had been thrown away."

Just the mention of Emma made Lucy cry. She pedaled fast, ahead of Rosie, concentrating only on the hills between Baker's Hollow and Charlottesville, not allowing herself to think about the news of Regina Blake's baby.

chapter twelve

No one was home at the Childs's. When Lucy and Rosie arrived just after four in the afternoon, there was a scribbled note, left by her parents, on the front door to Lucy: *"We'll be back at 3:30. M."*

But the house was empty. It looked as if they had left in a hurry. There were newspapers and coffee cups on the floor. Bolivar was dipping his paw into the pitcher on the kitchen table and delicately licking off the milk. Half a sandwich was on the counter. In the living room, Rosie found her mother's scarf on the arm of the couch.

"So my mother was here," she said, sinking into the couch.

Lucy sat in the chair across from Rosie and folded her legs underneath her.

"What do you suppose has happened?" Lucy asked.

Rosie shook her head.

"But they didn't plan for Dad to leave with the ransom money until close to eight," Lucy said. She was thinking she should tell her parents that the woman on the path in Baker's Hollow had told her the baby had disappeared. But if she was gone, Lucy was wondering, why would the woman have been so calm? And she had been calm.

"Maybe your parents heard something about the baby," Rosie said quietly.

Lucy didn't reply. For a long time they sat in the living room, silhouetted by a shaft of sunlight from the picture window just beyond where Rosie was sitting. The telephone rang and it was Rosie's sister Maud, asking where Mrs. Treeman was, why wasn't she home, and saying that Ian had broken the china teapot and Brendan probably had chicken pox.

"I suppose I should go home," Rosie said. "I'm going to be in terrible trouble because I said I was going to the Retirement Home with cookies."

But instead she sat back down on the couch, putting her head on the arm.

"I don't want you to go home now," Lucy said quietly. She had been sitting very still, hoping that the pounding of her heart would stop, that the picture of her baby with the peach-fuzz hair, wrapped in a yellow blanket as she last saw her, would disappear from the corner of her mind.

"What's the matter, Luce?" Rosie asked. Lucy's face looked stricken. Her dark eyes were wide and wet, her skin was pale. "What's happened?"

"I think something's happened to the baby," Lucy said. "I think she could be dead."

"Dead!" Rosie said. "How could she be dead? Your parents are giving Mr. Barnes a lot of money tonight to get her back. I'm sure she's fine."

"You know the woman I saw?"

"Of course," Rosie said.

"She said to me, 'I suppose you're looking for Regina's baby,' " Lucy said. "I didn't answer. So she said that Regina's baby had disappeared."

"Disappeared?"

"And then she said the baby could be dead."

"She said that?"

Lucy nodded.

"Oh, Lucy," Rosie said. "Why didn't you tell me in the first place? I wouldn't have complained so much about the bike."

"Maybe the woman was lying," Lucy said. "I think she knew who I was."

"I'm sure she was lying," Rosie said. "I simply know it's not true."

"Well, something is true," Lucy said.

"Of course," Rosie said. "It's true that Mr. Barnes stole your baby and is trying to get money from your parents before he'll give her back."

The telephone rang and it was Maud again, saying that Mr. Treeman was home now and wanted to know where everyone was—Rosie, in particular—and why the lunch dishes had not been done.

"Oh, brother," Rosie said, falling back into the couch.

"Should we tell my parents that we went to Regina Blake's when they come back?" Lucy asked.

"I don't know," Rosie said. "My mother thinks I'm at the Retirement Home."

"And my mother thinks I'm with you."

"We shouldn't tell," Rosie said.

"But what about the baby?" Lucy said. She heard a car turning into the driveway. "What do you think? Shouldn't we say something about the baby?"

"Like what?" Rosie asked.

"That we heard something bad might have happened to her. That we met a woman who could have been Regina."

"I didn't meet her," Rosie said. "And I certainly don't think something bad has happened to the baby."

"What should we say?" Lucy asked, watching her parents climb out of the car with Mrs. Treeman.

"We should say we were at the Retirement Home, Luce."

"Oh, brother, Rosie," Lucy said. "I can't believe such a model child as Rosemary Treeman has turned into a liar."

Rosie shrugged.

"I'm only telling a very small lie," she said. "And it's for a reason."

Mrs. Treeman took Rosie home.

"It's after four o'clock, Rosie. You've had plenty of time to go to the Retirement Home and be back to do the dishes."

Rosie rolled her eyes.

"I'm sorry," Lucy said to Mrs. Treeman. "It was my fault. We were just talking."

She hugged Rosie good-bye and heard Rosie whisper in her ear, "Call me as soon as you know something, and I'll meet you tomorrow after church."

Lucy smiled. Rosie had never, in all the years they had been best friends, missed church.

Dr. Childs was in a bad temper. He sat at the dining room table while Mrs. Childs made a pot of tea, and counted a very large stack of crisp fifty-dollar bills. The detective sat at the end of the table, his legs crossed, gazing out the window at the garden.

"What's the matter with Daddy?" Lucy asked her mother, who sat at the kitchen table eating a chocolate chip cookie. "Has anything else happened?"

"It's the whole situation," Mrs. Childs whispered, motioning for Lucy to come over and sit down with her. "We have been to take money out of the bank to pay ransom for this little baby, and the terrible thing is we can't be certain whether that dreadful Mr. Barnes will simply take the money and we'll never see the baby again," she said. "Daddy is very cross that we ever got involved. He was perfectly happy with just you and Bolivar and me." She looked wistfully at Lucy. "And really, so was I."

Lucy put her head down on her mother's arm. Perhaps, she thought, she should tell what had happened today. But then, if she did tell, if she really told them what the woman said about the baby, then what? Certainly if Dr. Childs knew that, he would not put money in the mailbox.

"How much money?" she asked her mother.

"Three thousand dollars," Mrs. Childs said. "It's quite a lot of money to take a chance on."

Lucy got a sugar cookie and went into the dining room, leaning against the chair next to her father. The detective smiled at her but he did not seem to be a talkative man. He returned to reading the classified section of the newspaper with Bolivar, who sat beside him.

"Do you think that I could go with you when you take the money?" Lucy asked. "I'd just be in the backseat."

"No," Dr. Childs said, putting the money into a sturdy, oversized envelope and licking the seal.

"We have to be very careful," the detective said,

looking up from the paper. "Your father will go alone. We have already posted police in the woods beyond the mailbox, and don't want to arouse the suspicions of Mr. Barnes by bringing a group."

"I'm not going," Mrs. Childs said, putting her arms around Lucy and kissing the top of her head.

"What do you think will happen?" Lucy asked.

"Your father will go to the mailbox and put in the envelope. I certainly assume that sooner or later Mr. Barnes will take the money out."

"And will you be watching for him?" Lucy asked.

"We will be watching," the detective said. "But it's going to be very dark and difficult to see without being seen first."

"Enough questions, Lucy," Dr. Childs said. "You ought to go practice the piano." Which is what Dr. Childs said to Lucy when he had enough of conversation.

chapter thirteen

NOTHING HAPPENED.

At 7:45, Dr. Childs left the house alone in his green Toyota Camry with the large envelope containing three thousand dollars in fifty-dollar bills. He returned home at 8:15.

Mrs. Childs had made pasta for dinner. She was just tossing lettuce for a salad when Dr. Childs walked in the door.

"What happened?" Mrs. Childs asked.

"Nothing," Dr. Childs said. "I drove down Route 29 just after the drugstore, and found a mailbox marked 'Kroger.' I put the envelope in the mailbox and did not even look around."

"What about the detective?"

"He parked across the highway, then walked to a place in the trees just opposite the mailbox," Dr. Childs said.

Lucy rested her head in her folded arms. The fear

and excitement of the last few hours had slipped away, and she was tired—too tired even to eat dinner—but she sat silently at the table while her parents talked about the possibilities.

Perhaps Mr. Barnes would pick up the money and call them to say he'd leave the baby under the Kroger mailbox so they could come get her. Or perhaps after he counted the money to make certain it was the right amount, he'd put Emma in his car and leave her on the Childs's front porch in a basket. Or perhaps Regina Blake would call and ask them to come pick Emma up.

Neither one of them mentioned the possibility that Emma would never reappear. And Dr. Childs, who had been so very glum about the baby, was full of hope.

Only Lucy had lost her enthusiasm.

"You're awfully quiet tonight, Lucy," Dr. Childs said.

She smiled wanly.

She had been thinking about the baby. Sometimes she thought of Emma lying in a cardboard box in the corner of Regina Blake's cabin, crying and crying. No one bothered to pick her up. Sometimes she thought of Regina Blake's mother. Surely she had a mother. And that mother, who had been capable enough to take care of Regina Blake when she was a baby, might be able to take care of Regina's baby. She did not imagine Emma dead.

"Do you think anyone is feeding her?" Lucy asked.

"Of course they're feeding her," Dr. Childs said.

"Otherwise she'd be screaming, darling," Mrs. Childs said. "They would not allow that to happen."

"But what if they did, and couldn't stand the screaming. Then what?" Lucy had a sudden and terrible picture in her mind's eye of the baby, left to scream in the woods beyond anyone's hearing.

"Someone will surely feed her, darling," Mrs. Childs said. "I promise."

At nine, Mrs. Treeman called to see what had happened when Dr. Childs took the money.

"When you're finished talking, could I speak to Rosie?" Lucy asked.

"Mrs. Treeman says that Rosie has gone to bed."

"I'm sure that's not true," Lucy said, resigned. "She's watching television and Mrs. Treeman just won't let her talk."

She picked up Bolivar and went into the living room, curled up on the bottom of the couch, and closed her eyes.

"Don't you want to go up to bed, Lucy?" Mrs. Childs asked.

"No," Lucy replied. "I'll wait here to see what happens."

▲   ▲   ▲

They waited for a long time.

"Wouldn't you think the detective would let us know something, Anthony?" Mrs. Childs asked.

"I would think," Dr. Childs replied.

But the detective did not return and he did not call. From time to time, Lucy slipped into a sad sleep, but mostly she lay on her side with Bolivar's large head under her chin and looked absently at the blue French chairs on the other side of the living room.

She was in one of her small sleeps, however, when the detective knocked on the front door. It had begun to rain and he apologized for his wet feet, for the rainwater splashing from his broad shoulders.

He lifted his arms in a gesture of frustration and shook his head.

"No one came," he told them. "I waited until it was completely dark, then I crossed the highway and went into the woods behind the mailbox so I could see better if anyone came to check the mailbox," he said. "Nothing." He checked his watch. "It's after midnight."

"Perhaps he saw you cross the highway," Dr. Childs said.

"Perhaps, but I don't think so," the detective said. "A police car with two officers is still there, but parked some distance away. We'll just have to wait.

Maybe there will be another message in the morning." He used the telephone in the kitchen to call his wife. "I'll see you first thing in the morning," he said to the Childses. "Chin up," he said to Lucy.

Lucy must have fallen asleep on the couch, because she didn't remember how she got from the living room to her bedroom and under the covers of her own bed. But she woke up very early with the sun streaming across her comforter and Bolivar sleeping soundly on her pillow.

Her parents were already downstairs, although it was only six-thirty on Sunday morning. Mrs. Childs looked as if she had not been to bed. They were not reading the Sunday paper as they absolutely always did first thing in the morning, and there was no breakfast—not even cereal or coffee on the kitchen table. Just a bottle of Evian water, from which Mrs. Childs was drinking when Lucy came in.

"Hi," Lucy said, taking the chair between them.

"Hello, Lucy," Dr. Childs said, in quite a warm, affectionate voice, which was surprising since Dr. Childs was often quite grumpy in the morning.

"Hello, darling," Mrs. Childs said, pushing a strand of hair out of Lucy's eyes.

"Anything happen?" Lucy asked.

"Not so far," Dr. Childs said. "I checked our own mailbox here this morning, and there is no note."

"What about the mailbox where you left the money?" Lucy asked.

"We haven't checked," Dr. Childs said. "I have already spoken to the detective this morning, and I'm leaving in just a few minutes to check that box. If the money is gone, then we will discuss what to do next."

It was raining, a light rain that fell in shafts of sunlight, giving the day the color of lavender. Dr. Childs left without his raincoat, got in his car, and drove out the driveway.

Lucy looked in the fridge. "It's really empty today, Mama," she said. "Not even any milk for cereal."

"Not even any cereal," Mrs. Childs said. "We'll go to the market when your father gets back."

"I'll go," Lucy said.

"But it's raining."

"Not very much," Lucy said, going up the steps to get dressed. "And I want to do something besides wait."

She put on jeans, a maroon turtleneck, and her sneakers, then brushed her fine hair and pulled it back in a ponytail.

"Want a raincoat?" Mrs. Childs asked, giving Lucy a twenty-dollar bill.

Lucy took her red slicker from the hook, kissed her mother, and started to leave.

"We need milk and orange juice and bread," Mrs. Childs said. "And maybe some of the yummy blueberry muffins."

The air was sweet with the smell of early spring on the trees and bushes, buds just beginning to open Charlie's Market was at the corner of Rugby and Main, a small family-owned grocery store with an old-fashioned soda fountain and sandwich bar. Mrs. Butterworth had just put hot blueberry muffins on the counter and Lucy bought three, then a diet Pepsi and bread for her mother, a small bottle of apple juice for her father, as well as milk and orange juice and cereal.

It was just after seven when Lucy left the market to go home. The streets were empty. She did not notice the small robin's-egg blue car parked across the street, until she was on her way up Rugby Road, halfway to her own house, eating her blueberry muffin as she walked.

And then the blue car pulled up beside her.

In the next instant a man jumped out of the car, pinned Lucy's arms behind her, pushed her in the backseat, and pressed her face to the floor so hard that the blueberry muffin crumbled all over it, then he sat on her back so she couldn't move.

"Okay, let's get out of here," the man said. The driver said nothing, but the car picked up speed. "Faster!" the man insisted.

"I'm going as fast as I can," a woman said, in a voice that Lucy recognized.

chapter fourteen

When Dr. Childs pulled in the driveway and got out of the car, Mrs. Childs was sitting on the front steps waiting for Lucy. The rain had stopped and the morning sun was breaking through the few cotton-puff clouds just above the trees.

"It's gone," he said. "The mailbox was empty."

He kissed Mrs. Childs on top of her head.

"Now the question is, what do we do?" he said, going in the house. Mrs. Childs followed him.

"Did you see Lucy on Rugby Road?"

"On Rugby?" he asked. "I didn't, but then I wasn't looking."

"She went to the market to buy some breakfast," Mrs. Childs said. "She left almost half an hour ago and I expected her back by now."

Dr. Childs checked his watch. "She'll be back soon," he said, and dialed the number for the detective at home.

"The mailbox was empty," he told him. "I checked this morning."

The detective said that the police had been unable to locate Mr. Barnes for questioning, but they did have information that someone of his general description was seen in a blue Honda with South Carolina license plates that morning near the University and the police were checking.

Dr. Childs opened the Sunday paper but he could not concentrate.

"Did you give her a long list for the market?" he asked Mrs. Childs.

"Not very," she said, sitting down on the arm of the chair where he was reading.

Rosie Treeman called and Mrs. Childs told her that Lucy was at the market and would call back. The detective called to say he was going to police headquarters and would be at the Childs's right afterward. When Dr. Childs got off the telephone, Mrs. Childs came into the kitchen, her arms folded tight across her chest.

"It's been almost forty-five minutes—unless she met a friend," she said.

"I'll call the market," Dr. Childs said, dialing Charlie's.

"She's come and gone," Mrs. Butterworth said, when Dr. Childs asked.

"Gone?" Dr. Childs asked.

"She's been gone for more than half an hour," Mrs. Butterworth said. "She got some hot blueberry

103

muffins. The last I saw of her, she was walking toward Rugby eating one of those muffins."

Dr. Childs thanked Mrs. Butterworth and put the phone down.

"I had a feeling," Mrs. Childs said. "I was afraid."

"We'll go out and look," Dr. Childs said. "I'm sure she's met up with someone on the way. Miss Terrell, perhaps. She's a constant talker."

"First we'll call the police." Mrs. Childs picked up the telephone and called the Chief of Police. Then she called the Treemans, asking would they come over because it looked as if Lucy had disappeared. And then she called the detective's house and spoke to his wife.

No one was on Rugby Road, except Professor Danzig walking his golden retriever. The Professor said no, he had not seen Lucy that morning, and Mrs. King on her way to early church had seen the Aiken twins on their bikes and Beryl Choice, but she had not seen Lucy—although, if she did, she would tell her to go straight home.

"She's gone," Mrs. Childs said. "I know it." She took Dr. Childs's hand. "I should not have been so stupid as to let her go to the market this morning."

chapter fifteen

LUCY LAY FACEDOWN IN THE BACK OF THE CAR, WITH her cheeks against the squashed blueberry muffin. The heat and the smell of gasoline on the floor carpet made her light-headed, and it was a struggle to breathe.

"Now what, Barney," the woman with a familiar voice said. At first it had sounded like the voice of the principal of Haddenfield Elementary, but of course it was not someone Lucy knew well. It was, however, someone whose voice she had heard before.

"Now shut up," the man called Barney said. He had a Southern accent and spoke softly with a lilt, like the sound of the voices of many of the fathers of her friends in Charlottesville.

"You want me to go straight to Washington, D.C.?" the woman asked. "Maybe we can pay a call on the President of the United States."

"I want you to turn left at Kroger's mailbox," the man said. He had his hand on Lucy's head, holding it close to the floor but without much pressure. She actually felt that she could scramble free. But if she did, then what? Then she would be in the car with these people and there was not much she could do about that, except jump out. He wasn't hurting her. In fact, the only discomfort she felt was the absence of air and the smell. She was afraid, certainly, but mostly she was concentrating too hard on breathing to think about fear.

The car turned into a bumpy road and slowed down.

"So?" the woman asked.

The man didn't answer. Lucy could feel him scrambling around in the backseat and then, in a quick movement, he tied a blindfold over her eyes and tied her ankles and wrists. He was actually almost gentle with her. "Don't scream," he said. "Nobody can hear you."

"If she screams, she gets a gag down her throat," the woman said.

"That's right," he said softly. "So you don't scream, okay?"

Lucy nodded.

"What kind of groceries has she got in the backseat, Barney?" the woman asked. "I could use some food. I didn't eat this morning."

The man called Barney rustled the grocery bag. "Milk, orange juice, blueberry muffins—"

"Give me one of those," the woman said.

The car turned again, slowed almost to a stop, then bumped along a road for a short while and finally did stop.

"We're taking you out now," the man said.

"Wait till I finish my muffin," the woman said.

"I can take her alone," the man said. "She's a skinny kid."

The door opened and he lifted Lucy out of the car. "I'm setting you on a bed inside a cabin," the man said, "and you're going to be here alone after a while, but we'll be back."

He walked in the door, carrying her under one arm. She heard the door slam behind them, and the smell of coffee and wood burning was strong inside the cool, damp room.

Lucy heard the woman's voice in the distance.

"Ask her if her parents are rich," she called out.

The man didn't reply.

"Your parents seem pretty well off to me," the woman said, in the room now. "A psychiatrist living in a big house."

"You're a stupid woman," the man said.

Lucy could hear his footsteps disappearing.

"I'm getting some coffee," he said.

She heard the rattling of pans and the low hum of conversation, then the slam of the door, the rev of the car engine, and then nothing.

She tried to sit up. She was on a bed or a couch

and although she did not recall that he had tied her to the bed, she seemed to be attached to a post so she could not pull away or stand up. But she was very glad they had decided not to gag her.

Her parents would be frantic. Her father, sharp tempered and reserved; her mother, weepy. The police ought to be there by now and the detective. Probably Rosie with her mother.

Lucy listened for the baby. She guessed that she was in Baker's Hollow where she and Rosie had been on Saturday. Maybe even in the cabin belonging to the Blakes, though she'd never seen it. Emma, if she was safe, ought to be somewhere nearby.

Listening, however, she heard only the slight whistle of dry leaves on the ground, the crack of branches, and the call of a bird—but nothing human.

And then she must have fallen asleep.

The next thing Lucy knew, she had the disconcerting sense that someone was in the room with her. She had not heard the door open, but she could feel a presence, like a ghost. There was a movement on the bare floor, a scuffling sound, and then it felt to Lucy as if someone was sitting down across from her because although there was silence she could feel breathing.

"Who is that?" she asked, facing where she thought the person might be, but not even the light of day came through the blindfold.

"Is it Barney?" she asked.

The person, if it was a person—it could of course have been an animal—did not reply. Lucy waited. There was no movement in the room, except once she heard the shuffling of feet again and an odd noise, like a large bird—not exactly a human sound.

"I wish you'd say something," Lucy said. And she waited.

"Anything," she said.

"Do you know about the baby?" she asked.

A wind had picked up outside, snapping the tree branches, singing through the window just behind Lucy, and she could no longer hear anyone.

"Did you answer about the baby?" she asked again, although she knew no one in the room had spoken. But she did think she could hear the sound of a baby crying or maybe it was the wind. She listened carefully. Certainly that was the sound of a baby in the distance.

"Are you a man or a woman?" Lucy asked.

There was a rustle across from Lucy, the sound

of wood on wood, perhaps a chair on the floor.

"A man?" Lucy asked.

"A girl," the person on the other side of the room said. And that was all she said for a very long time, but she didn't leave.

chapter sixteen

"I DON'T KNOW HOW ANYONE COULD HAVE COME TO the front door without our hearing them," Dr. Childs said to the group assembled in the living room at ten o'clock on Sunday morning, three hours after Lucy Childs had failed to come home from the market.

The group included Mrs. Childs, Rosie, Mrs. Treeman, Mr. Treeman, and Maudie Treeman, who was suffering from a mild case of chicken pox. Mr. Graham, the detective, was there, Mr. Horace, the Chief of Police for Charlottesville, and Ms. Smith, a policewoman who had arrived with him. Mrs. Butterworth from Charlie's Market was also there.

"We were talking, darling," Mrs. Childs said, stroking Bolivar, who sat quite happily in her lap, unaware of unusual trouble. "I don't think it's surprising we didn't hear anyone."

Dr. Childs opened the envelope that had been taped to the Childs's front door and handed the letter to the detective, who read it aloud.

We have yr. daughter and the groceries. You'll never see her again unless you put $3,000 in the Kroger mailbox by 4 p.m. today, Sunday.

Mrs. Treeman put her arm around Mrs. Childs. "It's too awful," she whispered.

"We're going to find her," Mr. Graham said. "We're going to find her and the baby."

"We must do something," Dr. Childs said weakly. "We really must do something now."

"The question is what," the police chief said. "The first thing, of course, is to send officers to Regina Blake's house in Baker's Hollow. But that is too dangerous."

"How dangerous is it?" Mrs. Childs asked. "We might frighten the kidnapper and then something could happen to Lucy, right?"

"That of course is the problem," Mr. Horace replied. "We do not know how dangerous the kidnappers are and therefore we must be very careful not to trap them."

The morning had become bright and sunny. Dr. Childs opened a window so that a soft breeze blew through the quiet living room.

"We never should have gotten involved with that baby in the first place," he said.

"It's my fault," Mrs. Childs said. "I should not have allowed Lucy to go to the market alone this morning."

"We're going to find them," the detective said, but his voice did not have a great deal of enthusiasm.

Mrs. Butterworth again repeated her story of how Lucy had come to the market that morning very early and bought milk and juice and granola low fat cereal and hot blueberry muffins. And then she had left at approximately 7:05, turning left on Main Street, and that was the last Mrs. Butterworth had seen of her.

While the grown-ups were talking, Rosie slipped into the basement. She sat down at the desk of the offices of Shrinks, Incorporated, and imagined what could have been going on in the mind of Mr. Barnes when he kidnapped Lucy. Besides money. Certainly he wanted money, and he knew that the Childses would pay any amount of money to have Lucy returned. But if they did pay the money and Lucy was returned safely, then what? Because then, of course, Lucy would know everything. She would know who Mr. Barnes was, and maybe where he lived, and she could probably lead the police to him. And that would be that for Mr. Barnes. It did not seem likely that a kidnapper like Mr. Barnes would be so stupid as to risk being caught. It seemed to Rosie much more likely that something terrible could happen to

Dr. Lucy Forever. She wished there were someone to talk to who would listen, but when she went upstairs the police chief had already gone and the Childses were leaving with the detective in his car to explore the area around Baker's Hollow. Mr. Treeman had gone and Mrs. Butterworth had returned to the market. Only Mrs. Treeman was left in the kitchen, making sandwiches for everyone when they came back. And Maudie was reading comics on the floor.

"It just breaks my heart," Mrs. Treeman said to Rosie. "And I feel so responsible." She spread mustard on rye bread. "This never would have happened if I had not stuck my nose in the Childs's business and let you tell Lucy about that baby."

"I would have told her anyway," Rosie said, sinking into the kitchen chair. "Lucy has wanted a baby sister since we were four."

She watched her mother slice tomatoes, then put turkey and lettuce onto the bread.

"Mama?" She didn't exactly know how to say it. "I'm really worried about Lucy," she began.

"Of course, darling. We are all worried about Lucy," Mrs. Treeman said.

"I mean I'm worried about the way the kidnappers are doing this," she said. "Lucy knows everything now. Why would Mr. Barnes let her go when she has seen the kidnappers? She might tell the police what she knows."

"Oh, Rosie," Mrs. Treeman said, leaning over the kitchen table, resting her chin in her hands. "You may be right, of course. I don't know what to say."

"They should try to rescue her without letting Mr. Barnes know," Rosie said. "I know where Regina Blake lives."

"They know where she lives too," Mrs. Treeman said. "They are going to drive over to Baker's Hollow."

"I know, I heard him say," Rosie said. "But they won't try to rescue her."

"We can't interfere, Rosie," Mrs. Treeman said, making lemonade. "The police are trained to deal with this and we aren't."

Rosie got up and went into the living room where Maudie was lying on the floor reading a comic.

"I heard what you said," Maudie said, flipping the page of the comic. "I think you should go yourself and look."

Rosie flopped on the couch.

"To Baker's Hollow?"

"To find Lucy."

"Maybe," Rosie said, going back to the kitchen where her mother was slicing sandwiches.

"Check to see if there are any cookies," Mrs.

Treeman said. "Although Mrs. Childs is not the sort of woman to make cookies and certainly, thin as she is, she doesn't eat them."

"There are always cookies," Rosie said, finding the cookie jar and arranging a plate of chocolate chips. She reached into the bottom cabinet and took out napkins, then took down plates. It gave her a sense of confidence and comfort to know the Childs house so well, to be more competent in it than her mother.

"They'll be hungry when they come back, poor things," Mrs. Treeman said, washing the mayonnaise off the knife.

"Is that all you need me for?" Rosie asked her mother, putting on a pot of water for tea.

"I'm just going to wait until they come back," Mrs. Treeman said, sitting down in a straight-back chair with the "Home" section of the newspaper.

"I think I'll go home, then," Rosie said, her mind spinning with a plan.

"That's a good idea, Rosie. You can help your grandmother with Ian and the baby," Mrs. Treeman said. "Maybe Maudie can go with you."

"I have a stomachache," Maudie called from the living room. "I don't want to go home with Rosie. I'll stay here with you."

Rosie went out the back door and around the side of the house to the shed where Lucy kept her bicycle. She lifted the rock where Mrs. Childs hid the key that opened the door, took out the bike, replaced the key, and headed down Rugby Road to Main.

As she turned onto Route 29, she had a rush of excitement, hardly able to believe that she, Rosemary Treeman, occasionally Miss Rosetree, was off on a dangerous mission without Lucy Forever or her mother or her brother Richie. She was going absolutely alone to save Lucy Childs.

chapter seventeen

LUCY SAT QUIETLY AGAINST THE WALL, TRYING TO
ignore the sharp pain from the rope around her wrists
and ankles. She didn't want to frighten the girl. She
wanted to say just the right thing to make a friend
of this stranger and so she was thoughtful, listening
for sounds of the baby, for the voices of Barney and
the woman returning, thinking what she could say
to make the girl trust her.

"My arms hurt a lot," she said finally, in an uncom-
plaining way. "They tied the ropes extremely tight."

There was no answer.

"You can see there are ropes, can't you?" she
asked. "They've tied my ankles too."

"I see," the girl said.

There was the sound of a car outside and Lucy
held her breath, listening.

"It's not them," the girl said. "If that's what
you're listening for."

"Do you know them?" Lucy asked.

The girl was quiet. She seemed to have gotten up and moved closer, because Lucy could feel her like wind.

"*I* have seen him before," Lucy continued. "And I think I have heard her voice."

"They aren't friends of mine," the girl said.

"Where am I?" Lucy asked.

"I know where you are," the girl said, but she did not seem inclined to say more. She sat as silent as stone until Lucy became afraid that she had offended her and the girl might leave. In fact, the girl had gotten up and was walking across the room when Lucy heard the baby crying.

"What's that?" Lucy asked.

The girl stopped.

"It sounds like an injured animal," Lucy said.

"It's not," the girl said.

"What is it?" Lucy asked. "I have no idea."

"It's a baby," the girl said.

Lucy's heart was beating fast. Blindfolded, with her sense of hearing more acute, she was certain that the sounds she heard came from Emma.

"Is it your baby?" Lucy asked.

The girl came back toward her and sat down on the bed. She touched Lucy's ankle.

"The ropes have made your ankles raw," she said. "But I can't untie you. They'd kill me."

The baby had stopped crying now, as suddenly as it had started, and Lucy leaned her head against the wall.

"Whose baby?" she asked.

"My mama's feeding it," the girl said. "But it's not her baby."

"Is it your cousin?" Lucy asked.

There was another long silence, but Lucy could tell the girl had more to say. Finally, she spoke.

"It's mine," she said.

Lucy could feel the blood rushing to her head in excitement and fear.

"So you're Regina Blake," Lucy said. "Do you know who I am?"

"I know everything," Regina Blake said.

chapter eighteen

ROSIE WAS NOT ATHLETIC. SHE WAS SMALL AND A little round with legs that her mother promised would grow, but they never seemed to grow at all. Even Maudie, eighteen months younger, was already taller than Rosie.

But Rosie was always stronger than she knew. For years, as the second oldest girl and the hardest worker in the Treeman family, she had been a second mother, working mornings before she went to school, and evenings and weekends, doing laundry, carrying babies, even scrubbing the kitchen floor after Sunday dinner.

She had more endurance than Lucy, although she was not aware of it. And besides, she had been born with the kind of stubborn temperament that would not quit. So she pedaled along Route 29, steadily without stopping, even though she was short of breath on the hills. It was 1:30 by her wrist watch when she turned right on Route 29.

The day had become pleasantly warm, the sun

almost directly overhead was bright, dappling the trees in young bud with sprinkles of light. Rosie found her mind wandering to the Major twins and whether Mrs. Major had halved their dress across the waist or down the middle and whether they had each gone to school in half a dress. The Major twins were spoiled and self-centered. They insisted on every new clothes fashion and fought constantly about needing new shorts at The Gap and a new shirt at The Banana Republic. Rosie had just begun to think about Mr. Braintree when she was conscious of a car behind her. The car must have been traveling very slowly, because it did not pass her bicycle. At first she thought people must have been looking for a turn but when it continued just behind her, even causing other cars to honk, Rosie alarmed, did not turn around. She was afraid that if she did, she would lose her balance. But her grip on the handles of Lucy's bike was tight.

Regina Blake leaned against the wall next to Lucy, close enough that their shoulders were touching.

"How old are you?" she asked.

"Twelve," Lucy said. "Twelve on November eighth."

"I'm fifteen," Regina said. "I don't want to be married. I want to go to high school and then get a job in New York City."

"What about your baby?" Lucy asked.

"I thought she was going to be fine," Regina said. "My baby was going to be adopted, maybe by your parents, and somebody was going to pay me some money for her so I could finish high school and quit my job at Burger King. And then this happened. It wasn't supposed to go like this."

"How was it supposed to go?" Lucy asked, pleased that Regina was finally talking.

"The baby was supposed to be paid for and I was supposed to get the money and that was all. That's what the woman told me."

The baby was crying again.

"She cries too much," Regina said crossly. "My mama says she ought to know better."

"I don't care about the crying," Lucy said. "I grew up without any babies and I wouldn't mind if a baby cried night and day."

"You'd mind," Regina said.

"Tell me about the man and the woman," Lucy asked.

"They're bad," Regina said. "That's all I know."

"Who are they?" Lucy said. "Do you know?"

"I can't tell you," Regina said. "If I tell, they'll kill me. That is what they said."

"Oh, brother," Lucy said.

"They told me if I cooperated, I'd get a lot of money—and a nice family for my baby," Regina said. "But I don't believe them anymore. They were just going to take the baby and give her back after they got the money. And then they got you, and now they haven't given the baby back to your parents or given me any of the money."

Lucy rested her head against the wall. She was too tired and hungry to be afraid, even when she heard a car pull up outside the cabin and Regina Blake jump up and run across the hardwood floor.

A new note from the kidnappers arrived at the Childs's at lunchtime, while Dr. and Mrs. Childs were picking at the sandwiches made by Mrs. Treeman and the private detective was on the telephone with the chief of police. They were not expecting another note, so they were surprised when the policewoman brought one in the front door.

> We are changing the amount to
> $5,000. Please be at the mailbox
> on time.

"A boy put this in the mailbox," the officer said.

"A boy?" Mrs. Childs asked.

"A young boy about seven or eight," she said. "I was waiting in my car, since we are watching your house, and along he comes, opens your mailbox, and sticks the note in."

Mrs. Childs put her head in her arms.

"Did you speak to the boy?" the detective asked.

"I asked him where he got the note, and he said a man in a blue car with a lady driving gave it to him, and gave him five dollars to walk down Rugby and put it in the mailbox marked 'Childs.' "

"Tricky guy," the detective said. "He probably knew we'd be parked outside the house checking on him."

Dr. Childs paced the kitchen floor, his arms folded across his chest. He was angry now and too worried to keep his temper.

"You have to find her," he said to the detective. "You have to find her by tonight."

But as he was speaking, Mrs. Treeman burst through the front door with Maudie by the hand.

"Has Rosie been back here?" she asked, out of breath. "Or called?"

Mrs. Childs shook her head.

"No," she said, handing the new note to Mrs. Treeman. "We haven't seen Rosie for quite a while."

Mrs. Treeman read the note and shook her head, sitting down in the chair next to Mrs. Childs, putting her arms around her shoulders.

"What about Rosie?" Mrs. Childs asked. "Didn't she go home?"

"She was supposed to go home, but she never got there," Mrs. Treeman said.

Rosie pedaled faster, even though her short legs ached from top to bottom. She could feel the car behind her, and with a growing sense of dread, she knew the car must have slowed down for a purpose, that the people in it wanted her. Just as she passed a long dirt road called Strawberry Path, the car slid along to pass her, so close she could feel the hot breeze from the engine. And suddenly, they turned into her bicycle and Rosie pitched forward over the handlebars into a ditch.

chapter nineteen

"THERE THEY ARE," REGINA CALLED FROM ACROSS the room. "I'm getting out of here."

But she didn't leave. Lucy could hear her creeping quickly back across the room, a soft shuffle and then she was beside her, breathing hot against her neck. Outside, Lucy heard the loud voice of Mr. Barnes and the woman shouting, "Shut up, Barney."

"Keep quiet," Regina whispered in Lucy's ear, and Lucy felt her untying her ankles first and then her wrists. "Now beat it," Regina whispered, and in a flash, she was gone.

When Lucy jumped up, ripping off the blindfold, the room was empty. Her heart was beating in her throat, her temples were throbbing. But the front door opened before she had a chance to look for a route of escape.

In the corner of the bedroom was a large bed and a smaller cot. Lucy slid under the large bed, pulling the skirt of the red plaid bedspread down so that it covered the space between the bed and the floor,

and hoped she was invisible. She heard them come in the room, the woman first, she could tell by the staccato tap of her heels, and then the man, in a terrible temper.

"So she's gone," the woman said. "You must have tied her with sewing thread."

"You know what I tied her with, and there's not a chance she could get loose."

"Then Regina did it," the woman said. "I bet you she came in here and undid the rope. I told you in the first place we couldn't trust that girl."

"Regina didn't do it," said the man, sitting down on the bed and sinking into Lucy's back. "Regina's too dumb and too scared."

"You don't have any sense about women or about who's smart and who's not," the woman said. "You're the one who's dumb. Not Regina." She made a loud sound like a sigh. "Now we're in a real fix. Real hot water."

Underneath the bed, Lucy held her breath. It was hot and tight and the pain of Barney, sitting on her back, was killing her.

"I wouldn't be so upset," the man said. "We've got the three thousand from the baby. I was against asking for more for the girl anyway. You're the greedy one," he said. "So now we've got more money than we had Friday and we'll take it and bolt."

"What about the baby?" the woman asked.

"Forget the baby," the man said. "Let's bolt now."

"You're such a chicken, Barney," the woman said. "I don't know how I could have ended up in business with such a chicken. And with me as smart as I am."

"Smart?" the man said. "Smart as a snake!" He got off the bed. "Smart as an alligator snake. So smart it never occurred to you that the mousy-haired girl is probably right in this room," he said. "And do you bother to look? Not a chance."

Lucy pressed her face into the hard floor.

She heard them walking, the woman's heels tap-tapping on the floor, stopping here, then there.

"So are you going to bother to look?" she asked.

"I'm looking," he said. "But we don't have much time. It's three already and that fat girl on the bike might have seen us. So I say we forget about the girl, head for the mailbox because we told them to be there at four o'clock, and head out of town."

"Ha!" Lucy felt a rush of air and a splash of light, as suddenly the bed moved back away from her head.

"See," the man said. "What did I say?"

The woman took Lucy by the wrist and pulled her to her feet. Lucy gasped.

"Tie her up, Barney," she said. "This time do it

right so she'll never see her parents again, or that little kid on the bike, either."

"Now that she's seen you, there's not much else to do but get rid of her, is there?" the man said.

They tied her hands and feet, but they didn't blindfold her this time. So Lucy sat at the end of the bed, looking directly at Mrs. Belgrade, the social worker from the welfare office of Albemarle County who had brought Emma to the Childs's house in the first place.

Mrs. Belgrade was not dressed up as she had been the first time Lucy saw her. She stood now in blue jeans and a flannel shirt, her hair tied up on the top of her head, with no makeup. The man, as Lucy had expected, was Mr. Barnes, who had come to the Childs's front door collecting for the Heart Fund.

"I imagine you're very surprised to see me, sweetheart," Mrs. Belgrade said to Lucy, reaching in her pocket and taking out a cigarette.

Lucy didn't reply.

"And I suppose you'd like to know where you are," she continued, taking a long drag on her cigarette. "This cabin belongs to Regina Blake and her mother. You almost got here yesterday but Regina intercepted you just a few yards from here. So," she asked, "are you surprised?"

"I'm surprised."

Mrs. Belgrade seemed pleased.

If she could just keep them talking, Lucy thought. But Mr. Barnes called from the next room. "Listen," he said, "we've got to get out of here fast."

Mrs. Belgrade cocked her head. "Bad news for you," she told Lucy, with a flicker of a smile.

chapter twenty

ROSIE TREEMAN ROLLED OVER ON HER STOMACH AND
sat up. Her arm was cut, not badly but it smarted,
and a little circle of blood spotted her gray Haddenfield Elementary sweatshirt. She checked her arms
and wrists, which she thought had been hurt when
she fell, but it wasn't until she stood up that she
realized it was her ankle she had injured.

When she took off her sneaker it was already
puffed out like a balloon.

Rosie Treeman was by nature a very careful girl.
She was good in emergencies because she was sensi-
ble and considered all the possibilities without making too quick a decision.

Now she sat on a rock, took off the T-shirt that
she'd worn over her turtleneck, tore it in strips, and
tied it tight around her ankle. It was three o'clock by
her Mickey Mouse wristwatch and soon Dr. Childs
would be arriving at the Kroger mailbox with the
money for Lucy. She must be very close to the turn-
off for Regina Blake's house, so if Lucy's bike was

not broken and her ankle cooperated, she could ride there.

She picked up the bike. Her ankle hurt and just the pain of it brought tears to her eyes, but she was determined. She climbed on the bike, a little shaky at first, and headed down Route 29 toward Baker's Hollow just ahead, hoping that Dr. Childs would drive by on his way to the mailbox and that together they would go find Lucy.

It was nearly three-thirty on Sunday afternoon, half an hour before the time that Dr. Childs was expected at the mailbox, just the moment that Rosie Treeman was pedaling painfully along Route 29 toward Baker's Hollow and Lucy Childs had been tied up for a second time, that the detective and the police chief decided to close in on Regina Blake's house.

"We know where Regina lives," Mr. Horace told Mrs. Childs. "We believe that in all likelihood Mr. Barnes will come to the mailbox sometime this evening to collect the money, and we are certain that he knows where Lucy and the baby are."

"We have a lot of police on stand-by," the police chief continued, "and one of our officers is disguised as a truck driver whose truck has broken down on the road just by the mailbox. When Mr. Barnes arrives to pick up the money, that officer will follow him."

"It doesn't feel safe," Mrs. Childs said.

"Nothing is safe, Mrs. Childs," the detective said. "We are trying to protect Lucy by not frightening them, so they don't do any harm to her—and at the same time, we want to find her."

And just as the officer got in his borrowed truck to drive toward Baker's Hollow, Mr. Barnes was dragging Lucy to the car, tossing her once again down on the floor in the back.

"Get in," he told Mrs. Belgrade.

"I'm driving," Mrs. Belgrade said. "What are we going to do?" she asked. "I think we ought to get out of here and forget the money."

"We're not forgetting the money," Mr. Barnes said. "We are driving down the road to the McDonald's and getting rid of the girl in the woods behind the parking lot. And then we're coming back for the money."

"And the police will be waiting for us," Mrs. Belgrade said. "What do you plan to do then, Barney, invite them to dinner?"

"I've got a plan," Mr. Barnes said. "You just get us out of here."

"You and your plans," Mrs. Belgrade said. "Do you have a plan to get rid of the girl?" she asked.

But Mr. Barnes didn't reply.

chapter twenty-one

IN THE DISTANCE ROSIE COULD SEE A WOMAN STANDING
in the clearing close to the turn for Baker's Hollow.
She pedaled faster along the flat path, her ankle
aching. As she got closer, she could see that the
woman carried a bundle on her shoulder, maybe a
baby, she thought. There were surprisingly few cars
along the road and though she kept her eyes on
each one as it passed, hoping to see the dark green
Toyota, she was already in full view of the woman
with the bundle and no one familiar had passed by.

The woman was holding a baby, a small yellow
bundle that was crying with the shrill cries of a newborn. The woman herself was young, with long
brown hair pulled back in a braid and denim overalls.

"Hi," Rose said.

"Hello," the woman said, avoiding having to look
directly at Rosie.

"Is that your baby?" she asked.

"No," the woman said.

"I've got a baby sister," Rosie said, getting off her

bike and leaning against the mailbox marked Kroger with a little thrill of fear rushing through her blood. "We always have a new baby in our family," she said trying to be pleasant. "Are you meeting someone?"

The young woman cocked her head but did not reply.

"I am," Rosie said. "I'm supposed to meet someone right here by this mailbox."

"Who?" the woman asked suspiciously.

"A doctor," Rosie said.

"A doctor?" the young woman asked. "There aren't any doctors around here. Who are you, anyway?"

"I'm Rosemary Treeman," Rosie said. "And I'm expecting a friend to be along anytime. Sort of an older man with an accent and he drives a green Toyota," she said. "Have you seen anyone like that?"

"If I was you," the young woman said, giving Rosie a level gaze, "I'd get out of here. There's going to be some trouble right here anytime now."

"Trouble?" Rosie asked.

"If I were you, I'd turn around and ride your bike back to where you came from."

Rosie sat down on a rock and felt her burning ankle.

"I would leave," she said to the young woman, "but I think I've broken my ankle."

The woman walked across the path to Baker's Hollow and leaned against an oak tree.

"I don't believe you about your ankle," the woman said.

Rosie held out her leg.

"See?" she said. "It's swollen nearly twice its size."

It was almost four o'clock by her watch. Surely Dr. Childs should be arriving any moment, unless something had happened. When she looked again at the young woman, she was talking to the baby, and it occurred to her that the baby could actually be Emma and this young woman could be Regina Blake.

"Can I see your baby?" Rosie asked casually. "I love babies."

"No," the woman said. "She's not my baby."

"I think I know you," Rosie said.

The woman shook her head.

"Maybe you're Regina Blake," Rosie said. "Is that who you are?"

"Who's Regina Blake?" the woman asked softly.

"It's who I think you are," Rosie said, astonished at her boldness.

And at that moment, Dr. Childs's green Toyota pulled into the lane by the road where Rosie was waiting.

Before Rosie had a chance to stand up so that Dr. Childs could see her, he was out of the car and had opened the mailbox. The girl stepped up to him.

"I know where your daughter is," she said quickly.

In a matter of seconds, Rosie Treeman and Regina Blake and the missing baby Emma were racing down the highway with Dr. Childs, followed by the officer in his borrowed truck and the chief of police, all on their way to McDonald's.

chapter twenty-two

"TELL ME EVERYTHING AGAIN," ROSIE SAID, LYING ON the brown couch which she and Dr. Forever used for patients of Shrinks, Incorporated. Her sprained ankle was propped up on a pillow.

"I've already told you twice," Lucy said, picking up the telephone on her desk. "Shrinks, Incorporated," she said. "No I'm very sorry but Miss Rosetree has broken her leg and will be hospitalized for another week."

"Please, Lucy," Rosie said taking a cookie from the plate behind the couch. "Everything, one more time."

"*Once* more," Lucy said and put her feet, swimming in her mother's black suede high-heeled shoes, on the desk.

Once more, Lucy told Rosie about Mr. Barnes and Mrs. Belgrade. How Mrs. Belgrade was a social worker who arranged for babies to be adopted and Mr. Barnes worked in her office. And how once they discovered that Dr. Childs wanted Regina Blake's

140

baby, they decided to kidnap the baby for money, since they thought Dr. Childs must have plenty to spend. It would be very easy and they had no intention of hurting the baby. They promised money to Regina Blake for helping them out, but in the end Regina was too stubborn to go along with their plan.

"And why did they kidnap you too?" Rosie asked, although she already knew the answer.

"Because they got greedy and thought, why not?"

"Did you think they were going to kill you?" Rosie asked.

"Not really," Lucy said. "They were not very good at kidnapping after all, and they just didn't seem the kind of people to do something that awful."

"Just sort of awful," Rosie said.

"But who knows what would have happened if Regina hadn't decided to save me?"

"What about me?"

Lucy laughed. "You were really the one who saved me, Rosie."

"Right," Rosie said happily.

Lucy picked up the telephone again. "Shrinks, Incorporated. Dr. Forever speaking."

"I'm sorry to interrupt you, Dr. Forever," Rosie said, "but your baby is crying."

And Lucy dropped the telephone, then ran upstairs to the kitchen where Emma, red-faced and screaming, had just woken up from her nap.

The afternoon was cool and sunny. A long ribbon of sunlight fell across the kitchen, across the crib where Emma had been sleeping. Lucy lifted the small, sweet-smelling baby in her arms.

"I can't believe she is actually going to be ours," Lucy said to her mother.

"Well, she is," Mrs. Childs said, heating Emma's bottle. "Regina Blake signed the papers today."

"Poor Regina," Lucy said.

"Regina is very happy to have such a nice family for her baby," Mrs. Childs said. "It was just not possible for her to keep Emma."

Lucy sat down in the new rocking chair they had just bought to rock Emma, took the bottle her mother had given her, and put the nipple in Emma's tiny mouth.

"So, Emma Childs," she said to the small bundle. "How does it feel to have Dr. Lucy Forever as your very own sister?"

And she rocked in and out of the shaft of sunlight while Emma lay happily in her arms.